"I'm not trying to rescue you, Jena.

"I care about the clinic and the shelter." Tucker paused. "I care about you, too."

"I know you do, but I have two months to come up with a solution. All I have to do is figure out how to buy that building and keep everything I love."

"*We*. I'm still your partner."

"You've got plenty of things to do, trying to move to Texas."

"I'm still in Rebel. Give me a chance to help?"

"I'm happy to have your assistance, but it's time I get used to being the boss." She turned her head when her name was called. "Excuse me, Tucker."

Before he could answer, Jena was across the room. He could only stare. Jena had gone from being overwhelmed to taking control of the situation. Almost as if she didn't need him. At all.

That thought caught him by surprise. Was he ready for the dynamics between him and Jena to change? He hadn't thought that far ahead, and maybe he should have.

Tina Radcliffe has been dreaming and scribbling for years. Originally from Western New York, she left home for a tour of duty with the US Army Security Agency stationed in Augsburg, Germany, and ended up in Tulsa, Oklahoma. Her past careers include certified oncology RN, library cataloger and pharmacy clerk. She recently moved from Denver, Colorado, to the Phoenix, Arizona, area, where she writes heartwarming and fun inspirational romance.

Books by Tina Radcliffe

Love Inspired

Hearts of Oklahoma

Finding the Road Home
Ready to Trust
His Holiday Prayer

Big Heart Ranch

Claiming Her Cowboy
Falling for the Cowgirl
Christmas with the Cowboy
Her Last Chance Cowboy

Rocky Mountain Reunion
Rocky Mountain Cowboy

Visit the Author Profile page
at Harlequin.com for more titles.

His Holiday Prayer

Tina Radcliffe

LOVE INSPIRED

INSPIRATIONAL ROMANCE

LOVE INSPIRED®

INSPIRATIONAL ROMANCE

Recycling programs for this product may not exist in your area.

ISBN-13: 978-1-335-55403-1

His Holiday Prayer

Copyright © 2020 by Tina M. Radcliffe

This edition published by arrangement with Harlequin Books S.A.

For questions and comments about the quality of this book, please contact us at CustomerService@Harlequin.com.

Love Inspired
22 Adelaide St. West, 40th Floor
Toronto, Ontario M5H 4E3, Canada
www.Harlequin.com

Printed in U.S.A.

Take therefore no thought for the morrow: for the morrow shall take thought for the things of itself. Sufficient unto the day is the evil thereof.
—*Matthew* 6:34

This book is dedicated to Chloe and Milo,
rescue cats who bless me daily
with their unconditional love.

Acknowledgments

Never underestimate the power of a writer
support team that believes in you
when you are hyperventilating.
Thank you, Tom, Sherri and Steph.

Thank you to my Wrangler Team for their support
with this new series, with a special shout-out
to Wrangler Dana Brown, who named the
ginger rescue cat in this book, Chester.

Thank you to reader Charlotte Barnett,
who shared the yummy pumpkin roll recipe
mentioned in this book.

A big thanks to Dr. Mike McConaughey
and the team at Acoma Animal Clinic
who care for the Radcliffe family pets with
compassion and wisdom. Dr. McConaughey was
kind enough to answer questions for this story.
All errors are mine.

Finally, thank you to my agent Jessica Alvarez,
who answers emails faster than a speeding bullet,
and my editor Dina Davis, who encourages me
to be the best writer I can be.

Chapter One

❦

"Looking good, Muffin." Jena Harper examined the suture line on the English bulldog, then removed her gloves with a snap. She gave the dog a gentle massage behind the ears before turning her over to the clinic technician.

"Any special orders, Dr. Harper?" Pilar Lopez asked.

"No, her incision looks great. Give the Tuttles a call and let them know their princess is ready to pick up." Jena glanced at the clock. "Remind them that the clinic closes early on Saturdays."

"Yes, ma'am."

"Thanks, Pilar. And thank you for working overtime until we find a second tech," Jena said.

"No problem, Doc. Mind if I take off after I call? My son has a scout meeting."

"Go ahead, and have a great rest of the weekend." Jena headed to the sink, scrubbed her hands and rinsed them before pushing through the swinging door to the staff area where her partner at Rebel Vet and Rescue, Tucker Rainbolt, stood at the counter in the file room, documenting in a patient chart.

"Thanks for handling those last few appointments, Tucker," she said.

He yawned and ran a hand through short, caramel-colored hair. "That's what I'm here for."

"Yes, but you already put in the entire morning out at Rebel Ranch treating that stallion."

"Small animals are a nice change of pace from the equine clinic. Hopefully Monday and Tuesday will be quiet for you, since I won't be around to help."

"Ah, yes. You're headed to Texas." She shook her head. "Explain to me why you'd want to speak at a university whose football team annihilated us this year?"

Tucker chuckled. "Life is not just about animals and Oklahoma State football, Jena."

She opened her lab coat to show off her OSU Cowboys black-and-orange sweatshirt, which managed to be both gaudy and tacky. "Says who?"

He stopped writing and looked at her. "You never cease to amaze me."

"I consider that a compliment."

"Don't you ever feel a little stifled in Rebel?" he asked.

"No. I love this town." Rebel was idyllic. Small

enough that you knew nearly everyone's name. Then from Memorial Day to Labor Day, the population swelled with tourists. There was always something going on thanks to nearby Rebel Lake and Keystone Lake. Yes, Rebel, Oklahoma, was pretty much perfect.

"Hmm," Tucker murmured. "I guess the difference is that you don't have two older brothers who hover over you at every turn."

"You have a supportive family who are concerned about your well-being. You're very fortunate." Tucker had no clue what it was like to have zero family, and she prayed he'd never know that feeling of being alone in the world.

"Yeah. Extremely fortunate," Tucker agreed. "But all that concern comes at a price." He released a slow breath. "I'll forever be the little brother. Even more so since we lost Levi and Megan."

Jena grimaced. It hadn't been her intention to bring up memories of those dark times when Tucker lost both his wife and his younger brother in separate incidents but so close together.

"It's not their fault," he said. "And it is getting better since both Reece and Mitch got married. Eventually, the folks in this town will ease off, too."

"The town?"

"Jena, the pastor's wife will pick up her dog shortly. When she does, she'll bring me a casserole. The woman has had my name on her out-reach calendar for over four years, since Megan passed. When I suggest removing me, she won't hear of it. Ridiculous, but there it is."

"Oh, wow. I had no idea. And I feel like a jerk of a friend for not noticing. I'm sorry, Tucker."

"Don't apologize. You're the only one who doesn't treat me with kid gloves."

She chuckled. "No, I can't say that I do." Often the two of them had running disagreements about all sorts of things. She definitely had no fear of telling him the truth about…pretty much everything. That's what made them such good friends. They could and did talk.

"Sometimes, I wonder if maybe there's something else out there for me." Tucker stared through the storefront window of the clinic as though he was a million miles away from Rebel.

Panic gripped Jena around the middle as the reality of his words sank in. "You're not thinking of leaving Rebel, are you?"

"Not at the moment."

"Good."

When the front door bells chimed, they both turned toward the sound.

Tucker followed Jena to the reception area just in time to see Saylor Tuttle sashay through the doggie entrance, holding a foil-covered pan and bringing with her the unmistakable scents of gardenia perfume and tomato sauce, along with a chilly late October breeze.

"Tucker," she said. "So glad you're still here." The pastor's wife slid the casserole onto the counter and then patted her sky-high, silver bouffant hair.

Turning slightly toward Jena, Tucker raised his brows with a 'see what I mean' expression.

"Thank you, Mrs. Tuttle." He smiled. "You know you can take me off the list any time now, right?"

"Nonsense. It's an honor for the ladies' outreach to assist you during this difficult time."

"Let me go get Muffin," he said.

"Muffin is healing nicely," Jena said to Mrs. Tuttle. "Keep the E-collar on to prevent her from messing with the incision line and continue cleaning the area as you have been."

The older woman leaned across the counter. "You know, honey, if you'd marry him, I could take him off my calendar."

"Excuse me?" Jena inched away from the desk, eyes rounding as she processed the woman's words. "Are you talking about Tucker?"

"Who else? He's a catch and you're the most likely candidate."

Jena took a breath. It wouldn't do to insult the pastor's wife, so she measured her response. "Tucker and I are friends. We went to college together and started the clinic together. I'm the twins' godmother." She raised a hand, then lowered it to the counter, still stunned. Never in a couple zillion years would she ruin their friendship and their professional bond by crossing that line.

Besides, she'd been burned in that arena and had no plans to let anyone close enough to be able to use her past against her again.

A soft bark from Muffin interrupted the conversation, and Tucker appeared from the kennel area with the English bulldog on a pink leash studded with sparkly rhinestones.

Still pondering Mrs. Tuttle's comments, Jena found herself staring at her partner as if she'd never seen him before. Sure, he was handsome. All the Rainbolt men were. Tall, with brown hair and deep blue eyes.

Tucker was a nice guy. She'd never paid much attention to the details because, as she reminded herself, they were only friends.

"There's my baby girl. Oh, my precious sweetheart," Mrs. Tuttle cooed. She rained kisses on the pooch and then looked up. "Thank you so much, Tucker. Muffin and I so appreciate you."

"Our pleasure, ma'am," he returned.

"Can you bill me?" she asked. "I grabbed the casserole and left my purse on the counter."

"No problem," Tucker said.

Jena shook her head as Muffin and her owner

left without a word to the other vet in the room. "You're welcome," she murmured.

"What was that?" Tucker asked.

"'What was that', he asks." She shook her head yet again and released a breath. "Ever notice how when you're around I sort of blend into the walls?"

"Naw, that's not true."

"Sure it is. Half our clientele comes in because of your charm and the good word from Rebel Ranch."

"And the other half?" he asked.

"We're the only vets in town."

"That's a glum attitude." Tucker lifted the foil on the casserole and peeked inside.

"Not from this side of the desk." Her stomach growled as the scent of tomato and basil drifted through the room. "That casserole smells amazing. I'm happy to take it off your hands."

"No way. While I may protest, I am grateful. Mrs. Tuttle is no slacker in the casserole department, and this is her special lasagna recipe." He grinned. "You're welcome to join me and the twins for dinner."

Any other time, Jena would be delighted to spend time with Tucker's sweet four-year-old daughters, but tonight she had special plans.

"I'll have to take a rain check. My book boyfriend and I have a long overdue date."

"Your who?"

"Book boyfriend." The only date she'd had in the last few years. With good reason.

"Book boyfriend?" Tucker asked.

"That means that the novel I put on hold at the library came in yesterday. Reading awaits me." Jena glanced at the clock. "In fact, I should have been out of here thirty minutes ago."

"You're right. And you would have been if we had hired another technician and a part-time receptionist."

"That I can agree with," she said. "We can't keep limping along like this. We have one receptionist handling calls for the rescue, the small animal clinic and the equine clinic out at Rebel Ranch. We're growing and we need help."

"I don't suppose there's been any response to the ad we put in the local papers?" Tucker asked.

"Not a nibble. Same as last month."

Tucker shrugged. "It's all going to work out, Jena—"

"It always does." She finished his sentence for him. "And you always say that."

"It's true."

Jena didn't answer. Tucker knew all too well that she wasn't the optimist he was. Instead, she turned around and searched the counters for the day's mail.

"What are you looking for?" He stared at the empty chair at the front desk. "And where is our long-suffering receptionist?"

"I told her to leave early. The woman hasn't had a Saturday off in months." Jena opened the desk drawer and then closed it. "She said there was an important piece of mail that came in." Lifting a chart, she spied a stack of envelopes. "Aha. Here it is."

Tucker moved closer. "That's from Slater Properties. Our lease renews next month. No doubt Charlie Slater wants to raise our rent again."

Jena tore the envelope open and skimmed the contents, her hand trembling. "Think again. Charlie wants to sell the building."

"What?" Tucker took the paper from her hands.

"He's had an offer from one of those veterinarian chains, but he's giving us first option." She looked up at him and swallowed hard. "What are we going to do?"

"Not panic, for starters. This is Charlie. As I recall, he wanted to sell the building last year, too. He told us it was because his sister was having surgery."

"He doesn't have a sister." They both said the words at the same time.

Jena couldn't help but smile, somewhat relieved.

"Charlie is bluffing," Tucker said. "The real estate market in Rebel moves slow. This is a tourist town. No one buys or rents here until summer."

"I bought your brother Mitch's house."

"That's different. You live here." He folded up

the letter and handed it to her. "Can you schedule a conference call with Charlie for next week, when I get back?"

"Sure," she murmured. "If you think it can wait that long."

"Jena, it's going to be okay. If worse comes to worst, we'll wrangle with that old codger until he agrees to something we can work with."

"Using the Rainbolt charm that you said doesn't exist?"

He released an embarrassed laugh. "Exactly."

"Then I hope it works this time, because there's not another available building in Rebel that can house both the clinic and the rescue."

"One day at a time, pal. I keep telling you."

"Right. One day at a time." Somewhere in the back of her mind, she recalled a Bible verse along those lines. Except right now, she was too stressed to remember what it was.

Once she'd logged off the computer and forwarded the phones, Jena traded her lab coat for a red wool winter coat and peeked out the front window. "What's with the weather?" she asked Tucker.

"I know," Tucker said. "Hasn't been this cold ushering in November in as long as I can remember. Though it's supposed to warm up this weekend." He pulled his lined denim jacket out of the closet and slid it on before reaching for his brown felt Stetson.

"Typical for Oklahoma," Jena said. At the front door, she turned the sign to Closed and flipped off the lights. "Always changing."

Tucker grabbed the casserole dish and followed her as she set the alarm and stepped outside. The streets of downtown Rebel were quiet for a Saturday afternoon. Overhead, the blue sky had created a backdrop behind the tall and barren redbud and maple trees that lined Rebel Avenue.

When another breeze whipped past, Jena shivered. "Brr." She tucked her hands into her pockets.

"You need a proper hat. That short pixie haircut leaves your ears without coverage."

She looked up at him, taking in his six-foot-two height. "Is it colder up there in the higher elevations?"

"Funny."

"For the record, I have plenty of hats," Jena said. "I'm just in denial that winter is on its way, which means Thanksgiving and Christmas will be here before we know it." She chuckled and turned toward Rebel Rescue next door.

"Aren't you going home?" he asked.

"I want to check in with my furry guests first."

"Okay, but don't forget to go home. You lose track of time when you go through that door."

"Five minutes," she said.

"Uh-huh. That's what you always say."

Jena couldn't help but smile. Tucker was right. She loved the rescue, possibly more than the clinic. Maybe it was because these animals needed her, really needed her. There was a therapy session to be had in that admission. Jena knew it and didn't for a minute deny the fact.

Like most of the animals in the clinic, Jena, too, had been abandoned. She'd been cast off by her parents and then taken in as a pregnant fifteen-year-old by her great-aunt, a widowed pastor's wife who understood God's mercy and grace far better than her now-estranged parents ever would.

She pushed open the door and stepped in. The air smelled of disinfectant from the day's last cleanup, completed by her staff of volunteers.

She greeted the matronly woman at the front desk. "Hi, Mabel. You're still here?"

"I was hoping to find a foster home for this feller before I left for the day."

Jena peeked behind the desk where a pup sat patiently. He cocked his head, his expression hopeful as he stared up at her. Floppy ears framed a light molasses face with white patches along the jawline. The furry body was mostly the same light brown with a white underbelly.

"What a sweet puppy," Jena said.

"Puppy? He's awfully big for a puppy, isn't he? Look at those paws."

Jena knelt down and offered her hand. The pup sniffed her, tail wagging furiously. "Not necessarily. Depends on which of his many relatives he's going to take after."

"What do you mean?"

"I think we're looking at a shepherd, golden, sheltie mix." She stared at the dog once more. "That's my guess."

"Is that the same as a mutt?"

"Shh. We don't want to offend." Jena gently assessed the animal's abdomen and extremities for injuries. "Appears to be in good shape. Can you hand me a reader, please?"

Mabel opened the drawer of the reception desk and pulled out a microchip scanner.

Jena wanded the animal and shook her head. "None, but not everyone microchips. We'll ask around and hopefully reunite this little girl with her owner."

"A girl! And you think she's lost?"

"Or dumped in Rebel." Jena sighed and stood up. "Who knows?"

She stared at the dog for a moment. Her eyes were so trusting. You could see into an animal's soul when you took time to look in their eyes. This one's gaze said, "I'll love you forever." Jena's heart ached because she knew that it was absolutely true. She rubbed the sweet spot behind the dog's ears. When the pup leaned against her, she knew she was in trouble.

Mabel glanced at the wall clock. "We're full up, Dr. Harper, and so are our foster homes."

A full house was both good and not so good. Great to be able to help so many animals, but it was definitely time to find furr-ever homes for each guest.

"Are there any problems that I need to check on before I leave?" she asked Mabel.

"No. Things are quiet. Pilar did rounds before she left for the day."

"Great."

"What am I going to do about this girl?" Mabel gestured toward the pup.

"Oh, Ernestine is going home with me." Jena didn't even think twice.

"Ernestine?"

"Doesn't that sound like a great name? I had a great-aunt Ernestine. I think it fits."

"You're so kindhearted, Dr. Harper."

"Have a good rest of your weekend, Mabel."

Mabel handed Jena a red leash and turned to the pup. "You don't know how blessed you are, young lady."

Blessed? Jena smiled at the comment. With all of her rescues, the animals gave much, much more than they received. Each and every one had rescued her. Yes, she was the one who was blessed.

Jena hooked the leash on the pup and headed out. "Come on, Ernie, let's go home."

Tucker's truck idled at a red light in the middle of downtown Rebel on Tuesday evening as he practiced delivering news that his partner wasn't going to want to hear.

"So, Jena, a funny thing happened at the conference." She had a good sense of humor, but this was no laughing matter.

First, he'd tell her how much working with her has meant to him. That was the truth. They were approaching seven years at the clinic, and then there was college before that.

Which was why he knew that once he explained that a prestigious Texas university had offered him a teaching position along with a list of perks to sweeten the pot, Jena would get it.

She'd be happy for him. If the situation was reversed, he'd be happy for her, too. Plenty happy. Jena had always been there for him, and he wanted only the best for his closest friend.

Hypocrite.

The unbidden thought ran through his mind. The truth was, he'd be happy for her and devastated that they were breaking up a great partnership.

He released a breath of frustration.

The timing was all kinds of lousy, too. She was already upset about Charlie's letter, and now he would deliver news that would absolutely derail life as she knew it.

Jena didn't talk about her past much, but there was one thing he was certain of. She liked change about as much as he did—or had.

Something had happened when the door to leaving Rebel opened in Texas. It was like a life preserver had been tossed his way. No one understood better than he did what it was like to walk through life with one foot in the past and one in the present. It wasn't working. He wasn't getting anywhere. It was time to move past his wife's death and slip out from beneath his brothers' thumbs. He prayed that Texas was the solution.

When the light turned green, a flash of red darted into his peripheral vision. Someone was running down the sidewalk of Main Street chasing a dog.

Whoa. It was Jena in her red wool coat.

Boy, she was fast. The animal was going at a good clip, too. A red leash waved in the air behind the little dog who appeared to be enjoying the chase.

Tucker drove around the block to First Street, pulled the truck over to the curb and got out, remaining hidden behind the front bumper. The dog was headed right for him, and when it neared, Tucker stepped out and grabbed the animal.

They both went down.

Tucker lay flat on his back on the sidewalk with a mass of golden, brown and white fur on his chest. The pup stared at him with big brown eyes. Then a pink tongue licked Tucker's face.

"Ugh, doggie halitosis."

A moment later, an out-of-breath Jena hovered over him. "Tucker, what are you doing here?"

"Laying on the sidewalk, apparently."

"Are you okay?" she panted.

"I'll live. Whose dog?"

"Ernie? Mine. Temporarily. The rescue is full."

Tucker rolled to his feet and handed Jena the leash. He brushed off his jeans. "It's possible Ernie needs obedience training."

"You think?"

"Yeah, I do. Throw in some dental hygiene while you're at it."

"Noted. Though in my defense, I haven't had time for a full exam. I've been a little busy since you've been gone." She looked up at Tucker and pointed toward his head. "You have a leaf in your hair."

He tunneled his fingers through his hair and shook his head. "Okay?"

"Yes." Her brown eyes crinkled with amusement. "I imagine you have a lump back there, too?"

"Naw, I landed posterior first and then we went down." He glanced at the dog. "Part golden?"

"And then some."

He nodded. "Lots of energy, too."

"That's an understatement. I thought I'd get an evening walk in. We've been running for three blocks."

"Is he from the rescue?"

"She. And the rescue is full. Ernie is my house-guest."

"You named him... I mean her, Ernie?"

"Short for Ernestine." Jena grinned. "After my late great-aunt."

"Ah. I see the resemblance."

She laughed, and the sound made him relax for a moment. "So, it looks like we need to find homes for your buddies, if the rescue is full," he said.

Jena's smile widened. She was clearly in good spirits. "Unless your family will take a few more."

"No way. The Rainbolts are bursting at the seams with rescue animals. Rebel Ranch took a cow and a goat. Daisy took that bonded pair of kittens. We gave Mitch a blind cat and an aged mutt. Even Reece took a cat, and I hear about that daily."

"Then it's time for an adoption event."

"I'll bring the girls. It'll be fun."

"Yes, it will be. I'll see if the community center will let us use their lobby again, then put an ad in *The Weekly Rebel.*" She pulled out her phone. "A week from next Saturday?"

"Great." Except he had a feeling things were about to nosedive from *great* real quick.

"Oh, and Charlie will call us Friday," Jena said. "I checked your schedule and we're both free at lunch. It's pizza day, so that works out perfectly."

Pizza day. They bought pizza for the staff on

Fridays and held an informal staff meeting to keep morale lifted and address concerns. He would miss pizza day if he left Rebel.

"When did you get back in town?" she asked.

"Just landed, and I was headed to your house."

"Oh?" She paused and cocked her head, really looking at him beneath the glow of the streetlamp. "Are you all right? You seem kind of... I don't know...off."

"Jet lag."

"It's a one-hour flight in the same time zone. You can't get jet lag in the same time zone."

"No?" He shrugged. "I don't sleep well in hotels, and I've got lots on my mind."

Jena chuckled. "I bet you texted the nanny every few hours checking on the twins."

"You got me." He glanced at his watch, becoming antsy under her cheerful scrutiny. "Speaking of the nanny, I've got to relieve her soon. Do you have time to chat? I have something I want to discuss."

"Sure. Absolutely."

"Do you want a ride?" he asked.

"We'll walk." She grinned. "I mean run."

Hands in his jacket pocket, he turned to his truck.

"Hey, Tucker."

He turned. "Yeah?"

Jena grinned. "Great to have you back."

"Thanks," he murmured as another dagger of guilt pricked him.

For a few moments he sat in his truck, once again working up the courage for what he had to do. He took a deep breath and put the keys in the ignition, praying for guidance at the same time.

Tucker's steps up the cobblestone walk to the cozy house seemed leaden. Forcing himself to think about anything but Jena, his gaze assessed her home. The one-story brick colonial was framed with climbing ivy, now more brown than green since the recent frost. In the front of the house, coral pots waited for spring, when they'd be filled to overflowing with blooms.

His big brother, Mitch, had done a lot of work on the house before he got married and sold the place to Jena. Therapy, he'd called it, and Tucker well understood. He'd done a lot of hands-on therapy himself.

He knocked on the door.

"It's open."

Although Jena shared her home with four cats and now a dog, the place smelled like vanilla and coffee beans, not animals. His gaze spanned the entrance and living room, noting that the place was tidier than his house, and he had a house-keeper. No layers of cat hair on the oak furniture, and the oversize moss-green corduroy fabric couch was stain-free. More than he could say for his own couch.

"What are you looking for?" she asked when she appeared in the living room.

"I'm not sure. Maybe the tiny robots who keep your house so clean."

Jena laughed. "I do have one of those robot floor-cleaner thingies."

Tucker nodded and glanced around once more. "They're doing a great job. Nice place."

"Haven't you been here before?"

"Yeah, when Mitch was in residence, but not since you moved in."

"I thought about a housewarming party," she said, leading him to the kitchen. "But I don't really do people stuff, as you well know."

"I do." He glanced around again. "Where are your animals?"

"Ernie is in the yard and the cats are in their room watching a squirrel video."

He blinked. "They have a room?"

"They do."

Sure they did, and really, why not? Animals came first in Jena's life. He knew that.

"Coffee?" she asked.

Tucker raised a hand. "I'm good."

"Have a cookie." She grabbed a bottle of water from the fridge and handed him one before placing a plate of perfectly formed chocolate chip cookies in front of him.

Tucker waited until she settled in a chair at the cozy circular kitchen table with its patchwork-design tablecloth before he sat down. Maybe if he pretended this was just a friendly social visit it wouldn't be so hard.

He grimaced. Right now he didn't feel much like a friend. After all, he was the one who'd practically begged Jena to come to Rebel to start the practice. Later, it was Jena who had held things together at the clinic while he walked through a thick fog of grief. Now he was going to abandon her.

"How was the conference?" Jena asked.

"Great. Really great." Tucker shook his head. How many times was he going to say the word *great*? Unscrewing the lid of the bottle, he downed a long swig. It failed to help his cottonmouth.

"So, what did you want to discuss?" She leaned forward, elbows on the table.

"How's everything at the clinic?" he countered.

"Same old." She inched the dish to her side of the table and carefully selected a cookie—the one with the most chips, he knew from past experience. Biting into it, she met his gaze. "Come on. Spill. What's up?"

"South Texas University offered me a teaching position." The words shot out of his mouth without preamble.

Jena gasped and then began to cough, jumping to her feet.

Tucker stood, nearly knocking his chair over, as his heart banged against his ribs. He opened her water bottle and shoved it in front of her. "You okay?"

With one hand on her chest and the other waving at him to keep his distance, Jena nodded and continued coughing, her face red with the effort and her eyes watering. With a final gasp, she reached for the water.

"Oh, my," she breathed. After another guzzle of the liquid, she sat down and wiped her eyes with her fingers.

Assured that she would be okay, Tucker sat down, too.

She looked at him. "I thought you went to a conference."

"I did."

Jena paled. "Who wants you to apply where?"

"South Texas University. They want me to teach full-time at the School of Veterinary Medicine."

Jena's jaw dropped. She was silent for a very long moment. Long enough to be a little scary.

"Teach what?" She narrowed her gaze. "Aren't you a little young for wool blazers and bow ties?"

"I'm as surprised as you. The emphasis in the program they want me for is rural equine veterinary medicine." He raised a palm. "Apparently, it's a big deal now."

Tucker half expected a joke about the long-standing football rivalry, but Jena wasn't smiling. Silence raged on as she stared at him. The only sound was the tail on the silly black cat wall clock swishing back and forth as the seconds passed.

"You said yes." Her words were barely a whisper.

"I said I'd think about it. And I am. Thinking and praying."

"What about our practice? The clinics and the rescue." Her eyes rounded, and she swallowed. "The animals?"

"I didn't say yes."

She blinked slowly, and once again was silent.

The silence stretched until he couldn't take it. "Jena?"

"When do they want an answer?" She met his eyes, and he flinched at the pain and confusion he saw in the brown depths, knowing he was responsible.

"As soon as possible, but they'll hold the position until January first. If I accept, they'll fly me down and move us into temporary housing."

"Wow, that fast?"

"The semester starts again in the middle of January. I have to set up childcare and prepare a curriculum and well… It's a big move."

"It's huge." She attempted a smile and failed.

Tucker leaned back in his chair and tried to sound matter-of-fact. "I'm sure we can find a solution here, somewhere, and we have two months to figure it out." He paused. "That's if I accept."

"A solution. In two months," she squeaked.

"You sound like you're freaking out."

Jena jerked back at the words as if coming out of a long sleep. Her chocolate eyes flashed with fire. "Yes. Of course I'm freaking out." She stood and paced the small kitchen. "I'm pretty sure I'm hyperventilating, too."

"I guess I didn't expect that."

Whirling around, she pinned him with her gaze. "What did you expect, Tucker? This is my life's work. My heart and soul. You're pulling the rug out from under me without notice."

He backpedaled. "If I had made a decision, then this would be notice. I'm telling you about the offer. That's all."

"Two months, Tucker. Two months."

She crossed her arms, effectively putting up a force field. Jena didn't get mad often, but when she did, he knew to approach with caution.

"Come on, Jena. No decisions have been made. Right now it's business as usual."

"I know you, Tucker. You've made up your mind." She stared at him, tight-lipped.

Tucker ran a hand over his face. He couldn't deny her words, and now he felt like the worst kind of friend. The lying kind. Lying to himself and her. He wanted to take the position.

At this point, there was probably no way he could spin this into something that she'd want to hear. He could only hope it wouldn't destroy their friendship.

Chapter Two

"Texas!"

Tucker's oldest brother Mitch's voice echoed through his thoughts as he flipped through the mail on his desk and booted up his computer.

This morning's family meeting hadn't gone as well as he had hoped. Both of his brothers had reacted like he was a kid who ought to have his mouth washed out with soap. Reece had stared at him while Mitch paced the conference room at Rebel Ranch. The hard footfalls of his cowboy boots on the tiled floor had been the only sound for minutes.

"You could teach at OSU if that's what you're hankering to do," Reece had said. "No need to go to Texas when your family is here."

"It's less than a five hour drive to the college," Tucker had returned.

"May as well be five hundred miles if you aren't in Rebel," Mitch had muttered.

"You're missing the point," Tucker had said. "It's a great opportunity, and yeah, it's not in Rebel, Oklahoma."

"What's wrong with Rebel?" Mitch had snapped, his voice rising. "This town has supported your clinic fine for the last seven years."

"Come on, Mitch. Sometimes people just need a change. Look at you. You gave up being Rebel's sheriff to help Reece manage the guest ranch. It was time." He had paused. "Maybe it's my time."

"Don't listen to them." His younger sister Kate's calm response had filled the room from the speaker function of the cell phone on the conference table. "Once the twins start school, you'll have to plant yourself in one place. Go to Texas. You can always come home if it doesn't work out."

"When is it you're coming home, little sis?" Mitch had asked Kate.

Their rodeo-loving sister had been on the road since she graduated from college, leaving her degree behind to follow her heart.

"I'm not in the hot seat. Tucker is," Kate had shot back.

The conversation had gone straight downhill from there.

A tap at his office door made Tucker look up from his desk.

Jena.

"We have that conference call with Charlie

at noon. That's in ten minutes," she said. Her brown-eyed gaze spanned the room, landing everywhere but directly on him.

Tucker glanced at his calendar. Was it only Friday? It seemed a lifetime ago he was in Texas. Yet it had only been a few days. "Noon. Yeah, right."

"Your office, I presume?" Her tone was all businesslike. Normally, she'd joke about the size of her own office, which was much smaller. Not today. One conversation and their usual teasing repartee seemed to have vanished.

Though he was in the clinic Wednesday afternoon, Jena had managed to dodge him since their Tuesday night discussion.

The expression on her face right now made it clear that there would be no joking on the agenda today.

"If you don't mind," he said.

"I'll be right back. I'm getting pizza."

Bring the old Jena with you, he wanted to say. Instead, he shook his head. The last time they'd been on the outs like this was when her loser fiancé had dumped her a few years back. She'd refused to even discuss what happened, and offering his concern had not proved helpful. If anything, it had caused her to retreat further for months. He suspected she still wasn't over that debacle.

Tucker reached for his cell phone once she returned with a paper plate of pizza in one hand

and a bottle of water in the other. Oversize black glasses were perched on the top of her head, and she had shed her lab coat.

The scent of anchovies tickled his nose, and he grimaced. Jena always had anchovies on her pizza while he preferred pineapple. They compromised by ordering half-and-half on one of the pizzas. Today, not even pineapple pizza could revive his appetite.

She put the water on the corner of his desk and wasted no time digging into her lunch.

"This month's Rebel Small Business Co-Op meeting is next Monday night," Tucker announced.

"Have fun," Jena returned without looking at him. She took another generous bite of pizza and wiped the sauce off her chin with a paper towel.

"They are fun. It's a good chance to compare notes with other business owners and the meal is always good. Luna Diaz, the ranch chef, caters dinner. You might enjoy yourself."

Jena flinched as if in pain. "That's a hard pass."

Her answer was no surprise. He'd tried to get her to attend the meetings and socialize with other Rebel business owners plenty of times in the past. Jena chose to hide behind the safety of her animals.

Tucker picked up his cell and dialed Slater Property Management. A moment later Charlie's voice boomed into the room.

"Hey, Doc."

"Got you on speaker, Charlie. Dr. Harper is here, as well."

"Great. Good afternoon to you both. Now how can I help my favorite tenants?"

"Favorite tenants?" Jena sputtered. "You sent us an eviction notice."

"Naw, I was giving you a heads-up that a bid came in for your building."

"I didn't know you were entertaining bids," Tucker said.

"Wasn't. This took me by surprise, too."

Jena frowned and leaned forward in her chair. "Mind if I ask who put in the offer?"

"It's no secret. Happy Pets. They're looking to extend their brand into Osage County."

Tucker grimaced at the words. Rebel Vet was doing well, but they were in no position to go up against a big bucks company like Happy Pets.

"The thing is, Doc, I'm about ready to retire. When I do, I don't want to have to drive into Rebel to check on why your air conditioner is cranky or your ceiling has a drip during the next downpour. This offer is looking mighty tasty to me."

"What's the deadline here, Charlie?" Tucker asked. "Keep in mind that in seven years, we've never been late on a payment and you've gotten free veterinary care on top of that."

"Point taken. Tell you what. Lease expires end

of November, but I'm willing to extend until the first of the year since I have a soft spot in my heart for you two." He chuckled. "My wife is going to tell me it's a soft spot in my head, but there you have it."

Shoulders sagging and head down, Jena was silent until the call ended. Their eyes connected and she tossed the remains of her pizza into the trash.

"Two months to sort through you leaving and Charlie hanging me out to dry," she murmured.

"I haven't left, Jena." Though even as he said the words aloud, Tucker put himself in her place. This was a double punch, and he hadn't planned it this way. He hadn't planned it at all, and he regretted putting his friend through this headache.

"I've been naive to think things would never change." She took a long breath. "I'm just trying to process this. I'd be lying if I said everything was fine in my world. It's not. And you know I'm lousy at pretending."

"I appreciate your honesty. I always have, but we have lots of options," Tucker said. "I'm guessing you thought about a buyback?"

"My bank account isn't prepared for that. I just bought a house. Would you consider installments?"

"Yeah. Sure. That's pretty much the way it usually works."

Jena rubbed her forehead. "I've got to find someone to take over the equine practice."

"There are options there, too. We can sell the equine practice."

"Finding an eligible candidate interested in the rural life is always challenging. In two months?" She shook her head. "Impossible."

Tucker couldn't disagree. The lure of country living was an acquired taste, as was the financial index. Sure, the cost of living was attractive. The salary by comparison, not so much. Finding someone who recognized that you have to take life in Rebel for what it is and not what you want it to be was the most difficult hurdle when it came to finding a candidate.

"Then there's the rescue." Jen released a breath. "I can run a solo practice but that won't leave time or money to support the rescue."

"You know," Tucker said. "We talked about doing a big holiday fundraiser for the rescue last year and then things just sort of went sideways around here when the twins got sick."

"I do remember Christmas," she murmured.

As did Tucker. There was little to be jolly about the season one year ago. Even the nanny had had the flu. If it wasn't for Jena lending a hand, he wasn't sure what he'd have done. Only a real friend steps in when everyone else is backing far away. Jena was a real friend.

Once again guilt slapped at him.

"What do you think?" he asked.

"The rescue needs funding. That's a fact. I'll give it some thought and see what I can get rolling."

"We. This isn't just about you. I keep telling you that I am here until the first of the year."

"You accepted their offer?"

He released a breath. "Not yet, but in truth, I can't think of a good reason not to."

She looked at him but didn't say the words he knew she was thinking. Jena wanted things to stay the same. That wasn't an option. He'd been stuck in neutral for far too long. He longed to move on to the next chapter of his life, whatever that might be.

"So in a perfect scenario," she finally said, "you'd leave for Texas and I'd take over the small animal clinic and another vet would cover the equine practice."

Tucker said nothing. Yeah, they both were thinking the same thing again. It was going to take a lot of prayer to make all the pieces of this plan fall into place.

"None of this addresses the building issue," Jena said. "January first, Happy Pets is going to come in and knock down Rebel Vet and Rescue and put up a shiny new brick-and-glass discount veterinary clinic." She released a breath. "I can move the practice somewhere else. Not in Rebel, because I can't compete with Happy Pets. But what about the rescue? All those displaced animals. It's not like I can shelter them in my living room while I transition to a new town and a new practice."

A pained expression crossed her face, once again slugging him in the gut.

"Two months," she repeated. "Thanksgiving and Christmas are almost here, and the first of the year is right behind."

"Maybe you could consider that we have two months to figure it out. Together, we can do that while enjoying the holidays."

"Tucker Rainbolt, the eternal optimist."

She was teasing him again, and that was a good sign. He couldn't help being an optimist. That attitude and the good Lord had gotten him through a series of dismal life events.

Jena continued. "Even with your eternal optimism, you cannot possibly think that you're going to spin this mess into snowflakes and holiday cheer."

"I'm not spinning. I believe there is a doable solution out there."

"Doable," she scoffed.

"Hey, if you don't expect much, you aren't going to get much."

Jena groaned. "Tucker Rainbolt happy quotes, too?"

"It's true and I call it as I see it."

She stood and paced in front of the desk, her brow furrowed with concern.

A knock sounded on the door, and Nolie stuck her head in. "Is this a bad time?"

"Yes, Magnolia, it's a bad time," Jena said without turning around.

Nolie's eyes rounded. No one called her by her given name.

"You two arguing?" she persisted.

"We're discussing," Jena said.

"That's code for arguing," the receptionist returned.

"Was there something you needed, Nolie?" Tucker asked.

"Dr. Harper's one o'clock cancelled."

Jena nodded. "Thanks."

When the door closed, Tucker ran a hand over his face before he dared to look at Jena again. "What are you thinking?"

She stared at him blankly. "What I'm thinking is that I need to call the bank and schedule an appointment immediately. Maybe I can take out a second mortgage on my house. It's time to consider all my options before Charlie sells the building to Happy Pets."

"That's not going to happen," Tucker said. "I won't let it."

"Tucker, this isn't your problem anymore." She gave a slow shake of her head. "All I want from you is your support as I try to raise the funds to keep the rescue operating. I don't know what will happen come January first, but I made a vow to every one of those animals when I took them in. I said I would keep them safe, and I plan to honor that pledge."

"Jena, I'll help you raise the funds for the rescue. I won't leave town until that happens. You have my word."

"Don't make promises you can't keep."

"You know me better than that," he said softly. He released a breath, disappointed that she thought so little of him after all their years of working together.

"I thought I knew you, Tucker," she said, cocking her head. "But never in a million years would I have guessed that you'd leave this town. You were the one who convinced me to come to Rebel."

He didn't know what to say to that. Once again, he felt like the villain.

She glanced at the wall clock and moved to the door. "I've got to get going."

"Jena, can we keep all of this between us... for now?"

"You don't want to tell the staff?"

"I don't want to tell anyone until we've got everything figured out. If our patients get wind of this thing, it's only going to make it more difficult to return to some sort of normal around here."

"Normal?" She chuckled. "Tucker, that puppy slipped the leash days ago."

"Maybe so, but you know what I mean."

"Have you told your family?" she asked.

"Yeah. This morning. So far, the only person who's had anything positive to say is my sister, Kate."

A long silence fell between them before Jena met his gaze and frowned.

"I'm being a lousy friend," she finally said. "I know I should support you in this. It is an amazing offer and career-wise, it's huge. No one deserves this more than you, Tucker." She offered a resigned sigh and stared out the window behind him.

"Thanks. That means a lot, Jena." He paused. "The thing is, I don't want to lose my best friend because of a job offer."

"Give me a few days to get over myself."

"Maybe you should take some time off."

"I just might do that."

Tucker sat staring at his desk calendar long after she left the room. For the first time since he returned from Texas on Tuesday, he was having second thoughts. Why had he thought this would be easy?

Was he wrong to promise Jena he'd make sure everything would work out? Optimism and faith were what carried him through a rocky childhood and a difficult past. Right now, the only thing he was sure of was that he'd started this bumpy ride, so it was his responsibility to get them to January first as painlessly as possible. Now he just had to figure out how to do that.

Jena stepped through the back door of the clinic on Monday with Ernie leading the way. Once unleashed, the dog headed to her bed right behind Nolie's desk, while Jena replaced her jacket with her lab coat and went to the kitchen to start a pot of coffee.

Her eyes widened when she moved to the reception area. From behind the reception desk, she scanned the waiting room. Cardboard turkeys, harvest corn and cornucopias dangled from the ceiling and danced in the air as the heater kicked on. A Thanksgiving wreath had been hung on the front door, and colorful leaves decorated the storefront window. Even the reception desk had been decorated and hosted a ceramic pilgrim family along with a plump painted turkey.

"Hello, Thanksgiving," Jena murmured.

"Like it?" Nolie asked.

Jena turned to see the receptionist huff into the room, dragging a step stool. "You've outdone yourself, Nolie." That was the truth.

"Thank you." She sighed. "Dr. Rainbolt had a somewhat different response when that hanging turkey poked him in the eye."

Jena chuckled. "He is tall."

Nolie stepped onto the stool. "I'm going to raise the fowl a bit higher."

"A wise plan." Jena examined the day's list of appointments Nolie had tacked to the bulletin board behind the desk. "Where is Dr. Rainbolt?"

"In his office. He asked not to be disturbed. Said he had to make some important phone calls."

"I see." Jena looked down the hall at his closed office door. He was no doubt making plans for the big career change. She rubbed her neck and tried not to think about the situation that occupied her days and nights of late.

"Everything okay with you and Dr. Rainbolt?" Nolie asked.

"Of course," Jena said.

"You two were having a pretty serious discussion at lunch on Friday. It didn't sound like everything was okay."

"It's not news that Tucker and I don't agree on everything."

Nolie cocked her head to assess the hanging decorations. "I got the impression the clinic is in trouble."

Jena jerked back at the words. "Why would you think such a thing?"

"I might have overhead you talking." She glanced at Jena and then looked away.

"Might have?" Jena stared at Nolie for a long moment. She debated pointing out that she ought to stop eavesdropping. But after sixty years, it was unlikely the plucky receptionist would change. "We're considering some restructuring," Jena finally said.

"Restructuring is code for I'm going to lose my job." Nolie offered a dramatic sigh. "I knew it."

"Don't even say that. If anything, I need you more than ever."

"I enjoy being needed." Nolie stepped down from the stool and patted her brassy hair. "Besides, no one likes to lose their jobs before the holidays."

"Nolie, no one will lose their job." Tucker might be leaving, but they weren't going to lose the building or the rescue. She wasn't going to allow any of that to happen.

"Yes, ma'am."

Jena glanced around. "Did you pull charts yet?"

"They're in my chair. Sorry, I got sidetracked when that turkey attacked Dr. Rainbolt."

"No problem." Jena scooped up the files and began a quick perusal of the recent notations.

"You okay, Dr. Harper?"

"Me?" Jena looked up. "Yes. Why?"

"You keep rubbing your neck."

"Do I? Just a crick." She smiled, dismissing the concern. "I must have slept at an awkward angle last night."

An awkward angle that involved her head on the kitchen table. She'd spent Sunday night running the numbers on her finances over and over, in an attempt to stop her life from imploding. Somewhere around 2:00 a.m. she had fallen asleep on the remains of a peanut butter and jelly sandwich, and she still didn't have a clear plan.

Jena stifled a groan as she stretched the protesting muscles.

"You know, a little mentholated cream will fix you right up." Nolie lifted the bifocals hanging on a chain around her neck to her nose as she settled behind the front desk computer.

"Yes, and then I'll smell like my great-aunt Ernestine."

"Better than a lot of smells we get around this place." She pulled a blue jar from her purse and handed it to Jena.

Jena took the jar and sniffed. "Point taken."

"By the way, Mrs. Saunders has called twice and left messages this morning. She wants to bring Milo in immediately, but only when Dr. Rainbolt is available."

"Is it an emergency?"

"No. Routine exam and vaccinations."

"Unless she wants to see the number two vet, who isn't tall, dark and handsome with blue eyes, Milo will have to take a number and wait until Dr. Rainbolt has an opening."

Nolie laughed. "I'll book her for Friday."

Jena glanced at the library book on the counter next to the ceramic turkey. It was hard to miss with its pink dust jacket and flamboyant gold script lettering. "What are you reading?"

"*Be a Boss*." Nolie reached for the book and handed it to Jena. "You certainly could take a lesson from the pages."

"Excuse me?" Leave it to Nolie to tell it like it is. Or how she thought it was. "What's that supposed to mean?"

"Honey, I've been here since the clinic opened. While it's clear that you're just as qualified as Dr. Rainbolt, you let him outshine you at every turn." She cocked her head and frowned. "Why, sometimes I believe you make him outshine you on purpose."

"I prefer to be in the background. Tucker is the face of the clinic because that's his personality. He's charming, and he loves people and they love him."

She'd said the words to herself over and over in the past until she believed them. So why was it that today they sounded hollow to her ears? Because the face of the clinic was leaving and she was ill-prepared to step into his shoes. Sure, she managed her personal life fine, because she had no personal life. But the business, well, that was Tucker's lane. He excelled one-on-one with the public. She excelled one-on-one with the animals.

"There's no good reason why you can't shine around here, too." Nolie paused. "Embrace your weaknesses as well as your strengths."

Jena thumbed through the book's table of contents. "What chapter is that?"

"Four. Right after, 'Be Your Best Self.'"

"My best self?" Jena asked. "What's my best self?"

Nolie lowered her bifocals and narrowed her eyes, giving Jena a critical once over. "You tell me. You're a makeover begging to happen with those sad fashion choices."

Sad? "Don't hold back, Nolie," Jena sputtered.

"Am I right?"

Jena glanced down at her faded olive green cargo pants and scruffy sneakers. Her long-sleeved black T-shirt was hidden beneath the folds of her lab coat. It would take no style awards, either. She resisted the urge to defend her wardrobe as being comfortable. Instead, she released a breath of defeat. "Is that what everyone thinks?"

"I doubt if they think about it at all. You manage to blend right into the background, which I assume is your goal."

Her goal? There was no goal. Personally or professionally. Therein lay the problem. Clothes, hair and makeup were an afterthought because her entire life for the past two years had been an afterthought.

"You've given me something to think about, Nolie." Jena slid the book back onto the counter.

"Dr. Harper, you're an amazing person. You know that, right?"

"I'm not sure, but thank you."

"You are and you are welcome," the receptionist said with an encouraging smile.

When the chimes on the front door sounded, both Jena and Nolie turned their heads. A petite young woman stepped into the clinic.

She wore a large army field coat, and combat boots peeked out from beneath the hem of a long, patterned skirt. A gray wool beanie did nothing to disguise the bright blue curls that framed her face—bright enough to necessitate a second glance. She had a perfectly oval face, brown eyes and scarlet Kewpie-doll lips. A pink Tupperware container was tucked under her arm.

"Excuse me, but there's a cat up a tree, right outside," she said.

"Show me." Jena followed her outside, with Nolie a few steps behind.

Jena peered through the leafless branches of a tall maple, her gaze landing on a long-haired orange tabby.

"Poor thing, looks terrified," the girl said.

"Why, that's just a kitten," Nolie added.

Jena nodded. "Looks like he's between four and six months." The animal clung to a horizontal bough as his soft pleading meow filled the air.

"Oh, baby. I'm coming. Hang on," Jena murmured.

"Why doesn't he climb down?" the young woman asked.

"Cats are built for climbing up," Jena said. "Their claws are like hooks, enabling them to scale trees easily. It's only when they arrive at their destination that they figure out that the descent doesn't work the same way."

"All cats go up and not down?"

Jena chuckled. "Oh, they can go down. This baby just hasn't learned how yet."

"Dr. Harper, do you want me to call the fire department?" Nolie asked.

Slipping off her lab coat, Jena handed it to the receptionist. "No, I have this."

"What do you mean, you have this?"

Jena swung around at the sound of Tucker's deep voice.

"One ginger cat up one maple tree. I got this." She cocked her head toward the tree.

Crossing his arms and frowning, Tucker assessed the situation. "Jena, let's call the Rebel Volunteer Fire Department."

"Oh, come on. Why should those fire jockeys get all the glory?"

"Because they have ladders?"

Jena blew a raspberry. "Give me ten fingers."

"What?"

"A boost." She nodded toward his hands. "I need a leg up."

"If anyone is climbing up a tree, it should be me." He raised a palm. "I'm taller."

"And heavier. That branch might not hold you." Jena stared him down.

"Fine," he muttered. "But let the record show that I think this is a very bad idea."

"Noted." She tapped her sneaker on the sidewalk. "Are you ready?"

Tucker grumbled something under his breath before he laced his fingers together, allowing Jena to step into his cupped hands. Then he raised her toward the lowest hanging limb.

Once she had wrapped her hands around a horizontal branch, she called out to Tucker, "Boost me up. I need to go higher."

"You better not fall."

"I'm not going to fall," she scoffed. "I've been climbing trees all my life."

Tucker grunted and pushed her high enough that she was able to straddle the branch while lying on her abdomen.

She pulled herself up until she could sit on the thick arm of the tree. With one hand against the trunk for balance, Jena stretched toward the kitten who perched on a bough above her head. "Come to mama, little ginger."

Her fingers were inches away from the orange fur ball who stared at her with wide green eyes, before deciding to back away.

"This is not going to work." With exaggerated slowness, she stood and then once again stretched out her fingers just as a rush of wind whipped past.

Jena swayed.

"Whoa."

She grabbed the trunk tightly.

Below her, a collective gasp sounded. Jena looked down and was surprised to discover that quite a few townspeople had collected. She recognized the reporter from *The Weekly Rebel* in the small crowd. Next to him, a few of her Rebel neighbors had phones aimed up the tree. One wrong step and she'd be a splat on the sidewalk and the video would go viral.

Not if she could help it.

She offered a silent prayer and then called down to Nolie. "Toss me a bag of cat treats. The smelly ones."

"Yes, ma'am."

A moment later, the receptionist returned and handed the bag to Tucker.

"Here you go," he called.

The package sailed through the air. Once it was high enough, Jena easily caught the bag. "Got it."

With her back against the trunk, she pulled out a few fishy treats, tucking the rest of the package into her pants pocket. "Here kitty, kitty," she cooed.

The kitten perked up, his freckled nose twitching. Interested, he inched toward Jena until he was close enough that she let the treats in her palm slip through her fingers and drop to the ground before grabbing the animal by the scruff.

"Got you!"

Below, the crowd remained still. All eyes were on her as she moved to a sitting position, with her back against the rough bark.

"Pass him down," Tucker said.

"Give me a minute." Jena soothed the animal, holding him snug against her chest. She patted gently, until a motorized purr sounded, and then pulled the rest of the treats from her pocket. The kitten's little pink tongue darted out to eagerly gobble up the offered pieces.

"We're ready," Jena called down. Kitty in one hand, she straddled the branch once again.

On the ground, Tucker, Nolie, Pilar and the blue-haired girl each held the sides of a blanket like a trampoline. Jena gently dropped the kitten into the makeshift life net.

Applause sounded from the crowd as Tucker pulled the kitten into his arms and cradled him against his shoulder. Rebel citizens crowded around, each eager for a glimpse of the orange tabby.

Minutes passed as Jena sat on the bough, plucking orange cat hairs from her shirt. She shivered as the wind picked up.

"Hello?" she finally called.

Tucker looked up and cringed. He handed the kitten off to Nolie. "Just drop. I've got you."

It only took a quick glance from Tucker to the

ground to have Jena reconsider what she was about to do.

"What's the problem?" Tucker called. "I thought this was your wheelhouse."

"Climbing yes. Jumping out of trees...not so much."

Tucker's lips twitched. "Maybe this would be a good time to call the fire department."

"No!" Jena reminded herself that she had trusted Tucker with her future for a long time now. This was no different. She closed her eyes and pushed off of the limb.

"Oomph." For a moment Jena froze, concentrating only on catching her breath as she lay encircled in Tucker's arms. Then she dared to peek up at him through her lashes and found herself mesmerized at the sight of the stubble of dark beard on his chin and his lips. When his gaze met hers, Jena's heart slammed into her chest.

"Are you all right?" he murmured.

Sure she was. Just a little light-headed, short of breath. And yes, her pulse was a bit erratic. But that was normal. After all, she had just jumped from a tree.

Yet, that didn't explain the funny stirring in her chest as she lay sheltered in Tucker's arms. As though she were protected...

Which, on second thought, is totally ridiculous.

In thirty-three years, she hadn't needed anyone. Except for one lapse. And look what that got her. A slap to the ego, when her fiancé realized she wasn't the perfect woman he'd placed on a pedestal of his own creation.

Jena stiffened. "Let me down, please."

"Yeah, right. Sorry."

Her feet touched the ground, and Jena took a quick step back to avoid brushing against Tucker. For long seconds they stared awkwardly at each other. The same confusion she felt a moment ago was reflected in his blue eyes.

What just happened?

"Thank you," she said softly.

"Sure." His cell began to ring, and he turned. "I've got a call."

"Yes. You better get that," Jena said. She adjusted her clothing, thankful that the crowd had dispersed.

"You saved him."

"What?" Jena turned to find the blue-haired young woman still standing on the sidewalk.

"You saved the kitten."

"Technically, you did, too. Thanks for letting us know."

"What will happen to him next?"

"We'll ask around to see if he belongs to someone. Otherwise we have a rescue right next door."

Their gaze connected and Jena paused as a flash of recognition struck her. How was it that she seemed familiar? "Have we met?" she asked.

"Not that I remember." The girl, too, seemed to falter for a moment. "I'm… I'm Dee Smith."

"Nice to meet you. I'm Dr. Harper."

"Yes. You're the reason I'm here."

Jena blinked. "I am?"

"That's not what I meant. The ad. I'm here about the job."

"Oh! Come on in." Jena held open the door to the clinic and Dee followed her in.

From his bed in the corner, Ernie got up and bumped her head against Jena's leg in a plea to be rubbed. Jena obliged, scratching her head. "So, Dee, which position is it you're applying for?"

"It doesn't matter. I'm not qualified for either, but I need a job and I'm enthusiastic and very hardworking."

Jena would have laughed aloud, but the girl was earnest, and the clinic was desperate for help. Instead she asked, "Do you live in Rebel?"

"Not yet. I'm looking for a place to stay, too." She dug in her tote and pulled out a folded paper. "My résumé."

Their hands collided, and the paper floated toward the ground where Ernie caught it mid-flight. Excited, the pup took a healthy chomp out of the paper.

"Oh, no, no!" Dee cried.

Jena snatched the paper from the dog, but she'd already chewed and swallowed a portion. "Don't worry. It won't hurt her."

"But my résumé."

"Nolie, can you find Dee an application?"

"Surely." Nolie stroked the kitten in her arms. "They're in the back. Let me drop little Chester here off in an exam room."

"Chester?" Jena asked.

"Doesn't he look like a Chester to you?" Nolie returned as she cuddled the ginger.

Jena laughed. "Chester, it is." Quickly skimming what was left of the résumé, she looked up at Dee. "College?"

"Accepted into OSU, but I had to leave due to financial constraints."

"I'm sorry to hear that."

"Me, too." Dee shrugged. "It's complicated."

Complicated. Okay, Jena could relate to that. *Complicated* described most of her life.

The receptionist came back with the form and handed it to Dee.

In a perfect world, Jena would go the official interview route. The situation at the clinic was far from perfect. They were desperate for help and the last time she'd checked, Dee Smith's face hadn't been on the wall of the post office as a wanted felon. Good enough for now.

"If your references and background check come back clean, Mrs. Parker will call and schedule you for an employee physical," Jena said.

"Background check?" Dee nibbled on a nail.

"A very basic one. It's standard procedure

working around medications and animals." Jena paused, assessing Dee's sudden nervousness and wondering if perhaps she'd made a huge error in judgment. "Is that a problem?"

"No. Not at all." She offered a wan smile. "I have secrets but none that are illegal."

"Great. I'll see you soon then."

"Yes. Thank you." Dee headed to the door and then turned back, offering up the pink plastic food container. "These are for you."

Jena took the Tupperware and looked at the young woman.

"Salted caramel brownies. They're my specialty."

"Wow. Do you bring all your prospective employers brownies?"

"This is the first time I've applied for a job." Dee offered a shy smile.

"Well, thank you," Jena said. Her first job application. She couldn't deny surprise at the admission.

"You're welcome," Dee returned. She turned to leave, and once again stopped. "Dr. Harper?"

"Yes?"

"Will you let me know if you don't find an owner for Chester?"

"I can do that."

The young woman's face brightened. "Thank you."

"Sure," Jena murmured. She stared at the door

long after it closed behind Dee, unable to shake the odd feeling that they'd met before.

"Are you going to hire her?" Nolie asked. She opened the plastic container and inspected the gooey treats. "She has zero experience."

"We haven't had a job candidate walk in that door in months," Jena said.

"There is that." Nolie narrowed her eyes.

"What can it hurt to give her a chance?"

"None, I suppose." Nolie paused. "What do you think of that blue hair?"

Jena shook her head. This was Rebel, Oklahoma. Most of the citizens only used landlines and believed Andy Griffith was a real sheriff. It was only during tourist season that the citizens got a whiff of the real world.

"Rebel Vet and Rescue does not discriminate based on hair color," Jena said to the receptionist. "We don't discriminate period. Besides, Pastor Tuttle's mama has blue hair. No one seems to find that unusual."

"Got me there." Nolie nodded toward the corner where Ernie now lay sprawled, belly-up on her red corduroy dog bed. Intermittent snores accompanied the office Muzak. "That one permanent, too?"

"Probably." Jena released a sigh.

Nolie gave a short nod, her eyes fixed on the brownies. She carefully removed a square from the container and took a bite. Her eyes rounded. "These should be illegal."

"That good?"

"They're amazing."

Jena slapped a palm on the counter. "Bake sale!"

"What?"

"I'm working on a fundraising plan for the rescue."

"I guess those grant forms we filled out last fall didn't come through?" Nolie asked.

"The ratio of applicants to grants is overwhelmingly not in our favor as a small-town rescue."

"If that's the case, then I'm guessing that you're going to have to think bigger than a bake sale if you're serious about a fundraiser." Nolie licked her fingers one by one.

"Any ideas?"

"The holidays are coming. When I was a kid and we lived in Tishomingo, my family went to a vet who had a Jingle Paws bazaar every year."

"Jingle Paws?" Excitement thrummed through Jena at the idea. "That's brilliant. But we need more than a bazaar. We need an entire event. Several days of fundraising holiday fun."

"I'm not sure I like that glint in your eye," Nolie said. "I get the distinct impression I'm going to be helping you with this brilliant idea of mine."

"I told you I needed you more than ever." Jena chuckled and headed toward the kitchen. "I never got my coffee this morning. I'm going to grab some and mull over this idea."

"Don't forget your lab coat." Nolie pulled it from her chair back and handed it to Jena.

"Thanks." As she passed Tucker's office, voices floated out to the hall.

"You can't afford to bail out the clinic if you're leaving town, and neither can Rebel Ranch."

Jena stopped at the sound of Reece Rainbolt's voice. Tucker's door was ajar, and his phone was apparently on speaker.

"I'm not trying to bail out the clinic. I don't see what the big deal is. We're financing the renovations at Ballard Farm."

"That directly funnels into the guest ranch. It's an investment that makes sense," Reece continued.

"The clinic is a great investment. The business has been in the black for seven years. Plus, it's prime real estate in downtown Rebel."

"All I see is a headache. I don't want to be a landlord. I've got enough on my plate."

"It's Rebel Vet and Rescue. Why is that a headache?"

"Because you're heading to Texas. That's why."

"I'm leaving in two months."

"That's my point. You're leaving town, so why buy a building in Rebel?"

Jena chastised herself for listening in, which

made her no better than Nolie. When she started to walk away, she heard her name and stopped.

"It's Jena, Reece. She's falling apart over this and it's my fault."

"You're not giving Jena enough credit. That woman doesn't need to be saved. Ever think that maybe you're knee-jerking because you feel guilty about leaving?"

Heat rushed to Jena's face, and she held her breath, frozen in place. The white lab coat in her hands slipped from her fingers to the floor. It was a moment of paralyzing clarity as the words between the brothers stabbed at her heart.

Nolie was right, she was the passive partner. She allowed…no, she had pushed Tucker into running the show. No wonder he wanted out, she'd been purposely riding his coattails for years, even more so the last twenty-four months, leaving everything but direct patient care to him. The man had taken on the entire burden of their joint venture because of her failure to step up and do her job. Now he felt guilty about leaving.

She grabbed her coat, retreated down the hall to her office and plopped down into her desk chair. When had she stopped participating in her own life? Since she'd been dumped by her fiancé after sharing her deepest secret—the fact that she'd had a baby as a teenager eighteen long years ago.

He'd claimed that Jena Harper wasn't the

woman he'd fallen in love with, so he'd turned on his heel and walked away. Three years of her life down the drain, along with what was left of her self-esteem.

Swiveling the chair around, Jena stared out the window. There was nothing to see except a few barren trees and an occasional car passing by on Second Street.

Her thoughts went back to the day that she landed on her great-aunt's doorstep. Aunt Ernestine had sat Jena down and said, *Pull up your socks.* Then she had patted her hand. *We learn from our mistakes and we move forward from this point on.*

That was what she planned to do in the next few days. Regroup, revise and redirect her life.

Tucker had suggested taking a few days off. That's exactly what she'd do. Take off Saturday and Monday. Focus on… What was it Nolie called her fundraising idea?

Jingle Paws.

Yes, Jingle Paws would be the start. It was an idea that held the potential to save both the rescue and herself. As for the rest? Well, she'd take it one day at a time and pray that the Lord gave her direction before Tucker left for good.

In the meantime, she had to figure out what to wear to the Rebel small-business meeting, because Monday night would be the launch of Jena 2.0.

Chapter Three

Tucker ran a hand over his newly shaved face and stared at the reflection in his bedroom mirror. The guy looking back at him was someone he didn't know anymore. Widower, father, brother, veterinarian. But where was he under all that? Who was Tucker Rainbolt anymore?

His faith remained unchanged, his prayers earnest. He wanted no more and no less than God's will for his life. Yet, each day the edgy restlessness grew.

Along with that, the gut feeling that something was off had loomed since Friday—ever since Jena flew out of that tree and landed in his arms. Looking into her eyes, something happened.

It was like when he'd dragged the jumper cables out to the barn and hooked them up to his grandfather's rusty 1950 Ford F1 truck. His brothers had laughed. After all, that truck had been buried in the barn for over twenty years. They said it would never turn over. Determined to prove them wrong, Tucker had spent weeks on the rust bucket. When he finally connected the cables to the battery and put the key in the ignition, the engine had coughed and sputtered before it came to life with an unexpected surge. For a brief moment on Friday, Tucker felt the same way.

Alive. It was something he hadn't felt in a very long time.

Alive terrified him.

Tucker grabbed his wallet from the bureau and paused before sliding it into his back pocket. Flipping it open, he stared at the picture that had occupied the sleeve at the front of the wallet for the last ten years.

Megan on their wedding day, laughing at the camera.

Like the photo, the sound of her laughter and her sweet whispers had faded. He blamed himself. The sounds he'd taken for granted lay beyond his grasp, like a heavy fog, only captured in his dreams. His brain said it was all part of saying goodbye. This was normal. If it was, then why was his heart heavy with guilt?

Swallowing past the emotion, Tucker headed to the living room to say goodnight to Ginger and Hazel. Tucker glanced around his small ranch home. He and Megan had had the house built when they had gotten married. Another plus for moving to Texas was getting out of this house. It held way too many memories.

"Time to give Daddy a kiss goodnight, girls."

His fraternal four-year-old twins wore matching flannel pajamas in pink patterns and were curled up on the couch on either side of the nanny, Mrs. Stewart, while she read a bedtime story. Sprawled across the back of the couch, Jesse James, their shorthair orange tabby, eyed Tucker with indifference.

"Daddy!" Redheaded, brown-eyed Ginger jumped up first and raced toward him, followed by fair-haired and blue-eyed Hazel.

"Me, too. Me, too." Hazel offered a shy smile as she raised her pudgy arms toward him.

Tucker gave each of his daughters a noisy kiss and whirled them in his arms, eliciting giggles of delight. When he inhaled the scent of soap and sweetness and saw the pure unconditional love that shone in their eyes, he was reminded of how blessed he was. His daughters were the balm that calmed the waves of anxiety that threatened at intervals over the last four years when he doubted his ability to be a good parent.

Thanks to the Lord, he'd been able to rise above his fear and pain in an effort to give the twins a normal childhood. That had been his goal, and he'd succeeded. Now it seemed that there was more out there. Tucker took a deep breath and straightened his tie.

Mrs. Stewart grinned. "Don't you look spiffy, Dr. Rainbolt. Do you have a date?"

"Naw. I'm just going to the small-business meeting."

"You know, I do have six granddaughters. Anytime you need a date..." She wiggled her eyebrows.

He smiled and bit back a laugh. Yeah, her granddaughters and Nolie's single daughter, and then Mrs. Tuttle had a list for him, as well. When he was ready, she'd said.

Was he ready? Wasn't that part of why he was going to Texas? To prove to himself that he was ready. Ready for a job, a new house and a new life?

He glanced around. "Where's Pugsley?" The roly-poly taupe rescue pug was usually in the middle of anything the girls were doing, sniffing and snorting, his corkscrew tail twitching.

"I let him out to do his thing," Mrs. Stewart said.

He glanced at the couch and noted a throw pillow with a gaping hole. "What happened?"

"That cat is what happened." She nodded toward Jesse James. "He was convinced the tassel on that pillow was a predator. I finally distracted him with a dish of tuna."

"You can toss it in the trash," Tucker said. The ugly tasseled pillow had been a wedding present.

The irony didn't escape him. Another piece of the past being disposed of.

"Daddy, can we have a piggyback ride before you go? Please. Please." Ginger tugged on his pant leg. His little redhead was the higher octane of the two. All energy and laughter.

"No, my sweet girl. I'm already late. Tomorrow. I'll be home early, and we can play."

Right now, he was on a mission to get to Luna Diaz's catered dinner as quickly as possible. Already his mouth watered thinking about the meal at the last meeting—eggplant rollatini, with an antipasto platter and three-cheese garlic bread.

Sure, he enjoyed the meeting and exchange of ideas with the locals. The presentation was always excellent. The speaker was either one of their own or an expert from Tulsa or Oklahoma City, discussing new marketing strategies or upcoming initiatives.

All good, but the highlight of the evening was Luna's gastronomic delights. If he got there early enough, Luna often gave him a to-go bag of baked treats for his daughters.

The Rebel Ranch chef spoiled all the Rainbolts like an indulgent aunt, something none of them had while growing up in a run-down trailer park on the shady side of Rebel. He checked his watch again and grabbed his coat.

"Be good for Mrs. Stewart," he admonished the twins as he turned to go. From the corner of his eye, he saw Ginger launch herself toward him and trip on her slippers. Down she went with a thud and a tangle of feet, face-planting on the carpet.

"Ginger!" Tucker reached for his daughter.

Once she started crying, a frightened Hazel joined in the melee. It took nearly forty-five minutes to settle them down again. Finally, Ginger was calm, sucking on a cherry ice pop to ease her bruised lip.

"Go, Dr. Rainbolt." Mrs. Stewart waved at him with a free hand as she handed Hazel an ice pop. "Quickly, while they're distracted. They'll be fine. I've got this."

Thank you, he mouthed back.

Halfway to town, he pulled his truck over to answer a call from an anxious pet owner who needed advice regarding their cat's eating behavior. Eye on the dash clock, he provided assurance and offered to add them to his morning house call list. House calls were part of the routine in the rural community and he liked the close relationship he had with his clients. Would he miss it once he left Rebel for a regular day job? Time would tell.

Right now, time was something he was out of. He stepped through the doors of the Davis Ballard Community Center, knowing he'd missed both dinner and the speaker's presentation.

Tucker glanced longingly at the buffet. The meal had been cleared from the service, but there was plenty of dessert. He wasted no time grabbing a plate and filling it with a generous slice of cherry tart. He savored a mouthful while observing a group of local business owners who had gathered near the podium, talking to someone. Tonight's speaker, no doubt.

Nez Eagle, who owned a local construction firm, laughed heartily at something, as did his sister, Melody, who owned Eagle Donuts, one of the most popular establishments in Rebel. Tucker recognized Mike Ross from Beep Jeep Tours standing close to the circle of the group. His over-bulked shoulders prevented Tucker from seeing who else was there. He shoved the rest of the tart in his mouth and tried to see past the shoulders from another angle.

"Let me fill your glass for you," Mike said to someone. When Mike turned, the seas parted, and Tucker was able to see the person in the center of the gathering.

Jena? Tucker blinked. It was Jena. In a dress. A dress that was a far cry from the baggy lab coat she'd been hiding beneath for years.

Half a dozen of the town's bachelors were doing their best to get her undivided attention. He couldn't do anything but stare, as an unsettling feeling stirred within him.

For the first time since they'd become friends, he was seeing Jena Harper as a woman, not his buddy. He turned toward the door, so stunned by the revelation that he was ready to walk out of the place, except Jena spotted him first and waved.

As she started across the room, Tucker's mind did a reboot, trying to reconcile the visual. Was this the same woman who attended Saturday church service so she could wear a hoodie and high-top sneakers? The one who'd passed on attending Reece's wedding as Tucker's plus-one because the event required her to get "gussied up"? Her words.

"Tucker. I was beginning to think you weren't going to make it."

"I…ah…" Tucker swallowed, his tongue thick and his mouth dry. He worked to pull himself together, determined to keep her from noticing he'd been flummoxed. "I didn't think so, either."

"You were right," she said. "Dinner was unbelievable. Luna served this amazing shrimp stir-fry along with these little dumpling things…" Jena gestured with a hand.

"Dim sum?"

"Yes, that's it."

He sighed. "What else?"

"Crab wontons." She shook her head and closed her eyes as if remembering. "Oh, and veggie spring rolls with peanut sauce. Amazing."

Tucker chased a solitary crumb around his plate with a finger. "Yeah. I bet."

"Luna peeked her head in and asked where

you were. She left a bag in the fridge for you to take home."

He brightened. "That was nice of her."

"It was. So why are you late?"

He met her gaze and looked her up and down, confused. "Why are you so tall?"

"Heels." She raised a leg. "I had my doubts about walking in these, but it turns out I can."

Tucker looked at her legs and then froze. "I, ah, right." He quickly glanced away. Was he supposed to notice her legs? This was Jena, after all. What was the protocol when your best friend morphed into a femme fatale?

"So, why were you late?" she asked.

"The twins." Her face registered concern as he explained. Jena loved his girls as much as he did.

"Poor sweetie," she murmured.

"She'll be fine and showing off her bruised chin on Saturday at the adoption event." He looked around the room. "So who was the speaker tonight?"

"Me."

"You!" For seven years he'd been trying to get her to a meeting. Tonight she was the speaker?

Jena nodded as though she'd read his mind. "Can you believe it? It was serendipity. I called your group's president."

"It's your group, too. The clinic pays dues to participate in the co-op."

"True. I just never realized what a nice bunch

they are. And so helpful." When she shook her head, he found himself mesmerized as the silver hoops in her ears swung. She paused. "Are you all right?"

"Yeah. Yeah. Go on."

She frowned as if doubtful. "Well, I called Nez Eagle and asked if it was okay to share some brochures at the meeting. He said the scheduled speaker was ill and asked if I wanted to speak." Jena shrugged. "I thought, why not? I had a PowerPoint presentation and everything."

"You were the speaker tonight, and you're wearing a dress." Tucker blinked once more, trying to make sense of the fact that his friend and die-hard introvert volunteered to be tonight's speaker.

"Yes. I am." She smiled. "You aren't the only one ready for change."

"You look nice, Jena," he murmured. If this was how she planned to change, he was all for the move.

"Thanks." She paused. "Don't you want to know what I spoke on?"

"I'm afraid to ask. I thought you hated public speaking."

"I do. Until I realized I could talk about something I'm passionate about—shelter animals. I just kept thinking about Ernie and Chester while I spoke."

"That was your topic?"

"Yes. I talked about a wonderful fundraising opportunity that all the local businesses will be able to participate in to bring in the holidays for our furry friends. Jingle Paws."

"Jingle Paws?" Tucker stared at her, trying to process her words and her appearance, and failing at both. "What exactly is that?"

"It's the holiday fundraising event for the rescue. Our first annual Jingle Paws."

"We have a holiday fundraiser?"

"Nolie came up with the idea. I sort of ran with it."

"Jingle Paws. I like the name."

"Me, too." She smiled. "Oh, and I hired a technician. The young woman with the blue hair who helped us rescue that ginger tabby."

"You already hired her?" The admission took him by surprise. Usually, Jena moved slowly when it came to making decisions.

"Pending a background check." Jena straightened her shoulders. "So I guess that would be a yes. Yes. I've pretty much hired her."

"She's experienced?" he asked.

"Not exactly, but she's sharp and… I don't know…it just felt right."

"Probably a good thing you didn't let her go. No telling when another candidate will come along until college is out in the spring."

"My thoughts exactly." She handed him a brochure.

Tucker slid his empty plate on a table before he perused the trifold color advertisement. "You created this?" The glossy brochure looked professional and eye-catching.

"I promised the printer one free well-checkup in exchange for printing costs."

"It looks great." He nodded. "Two-day event, huh?"

"Yes. The Ballard Community Center is donating space for free. Participating businesses will be charged a table fee, and so far the interest has been overwhelming. Mike from Beep Jeep Tours has encouraged everyone to donate a portion of their proceeds to the cause."

Tucker's gaze spanned the room until he spotted Mike Ross watching them. "Isn't he married?"

"I believe he was engaged, and they called it off. Why?"

"No good reason." No reason except Tucker didn't care for the guy. He was a little too tanned and toned, and he had his eye on Jena. Not good. Jena had lousy instincts when it came to men. Maybe if Tucker had had the guts to chat with her about the loser who dumped her a few years ago, he could have saved her a heartache. As her friend, he had an obligation to screen the playing field, and he intended to do so this time.

"What do you think?" she asked.

"About Mike?"

"No. About the event. I've never organized anything this big before."

"Pet fashion show and sale." He turned the brochure over. "A dinner dance and silent auction?"

"That will be held on a Friday night. Luna Diaz is waiving her fees. We'll just pay for the food from the ticket sales."

We? Now they were *we* again?

Tucker looked up from the brochure and into Jena's eyes. There was a soft glow to her skin and her lids had been shadowed, making her brown eyes appear even bigger. Was she wearing makeup, too?

"Why are you looking at me like a bug on the windshield?"

"Sorry. I was thinking. Lots on my mind." He nodded and put on a smile. "This is great. You've accomplished all this with a few days off?"

"It's amazing how enterprising you can be when your back is to the wall and desperation meets you coming and going. I haven't figured out how to save the building yet, but I hope to have enough funding to keep the rescue stocked with supplies and food, wherever we land."

"The situation isn't desperate," Tucker said.

"It is if I'm doing public speaking."

"I'm working on a few plans myself."

Jena tensed, and she shook her head firmly. "I will not be bailed out by Rebel Ranch."

Tucker jerked back, surprised and more than a little concerned. "Who told you that?"

"No one. I heard you and Reece talking."

"You were eavesdropping?"

"No, I walked by on the way to the kitchen and I heard my name and stopped. Actually, I didn't hear the entire conversation. Just enough to make me see that Reece was right. Rescuing me is not part of your job."

"I'm not trying to rescue you, Jena. I care about the clinic and the shelter." He paused. "I care about you, too."

"I know you do, but it's time for me to step up. Besides, you're right. I have two months to come up with a solution. All I have to do is figure out how to buy that building and keep everything I love." She paused. "I'm working on that part."

"*We.* I'm still your partner."

"You've got plenty of things to do, trying to get your life in order to move to Texas."

"I'm still in Rebel. Give me a chance to help, would you?"

"I'm happy to have your assistance, but make no mistake, I'm running things. It's time for me to get used to being the boss."

"You've always been the boss."

"Let me clarify. It's time for me to lead instead of follow."

She turned her head when her name was called.

"Excuse, me, Tucker. I promised I would talk about the silent auction with a few people."

Before he could answer, Jena was across the room. He could only stare, trying to figure out what happened since last Friday. Jena had gone from being overwhelmed to taking control of the situation. Almost as if she didn't need him. At all.

That thought caught him by surprise. Was he ready for the dynamics between himself and Jena to change? He hadn't thought that far ahead, and maybe he should have.

Tucker ran a hand over his face. Eight weeks until he left for Texas. He suspected they were going to be a very interesting eight weeks.

When a cold, wet dog nose pushed against Jena's face, she rolled over and landed on the oak floor. Confused and shivering, she sat in a tangle of sheets and blanket, staring at Ernie.

The dog licked her face and barked.

"Let me wake up, first, girl. Then I'll feed you."

The face in the bathroom mirror had black splotches under her eyes. She had memorized the vaccination dates of all her pets, but couldn't remember that mascara was supposed to be washed off before bed.

Another yawn escaped as she reached for a washcloth. Even after a full night's sleep she was drained. Limp as her great-aunt's egg noodles. This was why she didn't 'people.' Peopling sucked the lifeblood out of her. While it had been entertaining to be the center of attention during the co-op meeting, the fun had been short-lived. Jena Harper was an introvert. Period.

Her cell phone rang, and she reached for it. "Good morning, Nolie."

"Dr. Harper, Mike from Beep Jeep Tours called and is trying to schedule lunch with you. Something about the fundraiser? Shall I give him your cell number?"

"Absolutely not. I'll return his call when I get to the office." Good old Mike had shown more interest in her than in the Jingle Paws project. Not what she had had in mind at all. Somehow she'd redirect his enthusiasm into helping the animals.

Nolie cleared her throat. "When might that be?"

"What time is it?"

"Eight a.m."

"I guess I hit snooze one too many times," Jena returned. She wiped the last traces of sleep from her eyes.

"Are you all right, Dr. Harper?"

"You seem to ask me that a lot lately."

"Well, that's because you're acting strange." Nolie paused. "You took two days off out of the blue. That's a first. Don't get me wrong, I'm glad you did. I've often worried that you'll end up with compassion fatigue. But Dr. Harper, in seven years, you've never been late." She paused to take a breath. "Are you sure you're all right?"

"I'm fine, Nolie." As fine as she could possibly be, considering the circumstances. "When is my first appointment?"

"Nine-thirty."

"I'll be there very quickly."

Jena showered and reached for a sweatshirt and black jeans. Then she paused. "Nope. You are the new and improved Jena. You are the boss and you're going to dress like one." She released a breath. "Even if it kills you."

Dressed in slacks and a sweater set, she raced around the house feeding the animals before she opened the closed-in back porch or as she called it, the 'catio,' for the day. This was where her cats spent most of their time, watching the squirrels and rabbits in the backyard from a safe and heated enclosure with access to the house from a doggie door.

"Ernie, are you coming with me?" She dangled the leash, and the pup trotted obediently to the front door.

The town of Rebel was waking as she and Ernie raced down the street. Last night's frost was still evident in the sidewalk cracks, lightly covering the patches of grass in front of the houses along Oak Road and on the solitary brown leaves that still clung to the trees. Her breath came out in frosty puffs as they breezed around the corner onto Second Street.

When they reached the clinic, there was still time for coffee before her first appointment. Jena pulled open the door and came face to face with Tucker in the hallway.

"Oh, um, hi," she said. "On your way out?"

"Hey, Ernie." Tucker grinned and rubbed the dog's head. "Yeah, I've got a few house calls this morning."

"Have a good day," Jena said.

When he brushed past her, she could smell the faint, familiar trace of aftershave. He smelled good.

"You, too. Maybe we can find time to talk about Jingle Paws this week."

"Absolutely," she returned a little too brightly. Was she trying to convince Tucker or herself that it was business as usual?

Tucker stared at her for a brief moment and then nodded. He was out the door when it hit her. Come January, she'd never see him in this hallway again. Ever. As she slipped off her coat, a knot formed in her chest and she tried to breathe past it.

"Dr. Harper."

Jena whirled around. "Yes, Nolie?"

"Officer Gallegos stopped by to see you." Nolie held up a box of Eagle donuts. "I think you have an admirer." The receptionist grinned broadly.

"What?" Jena blinked. "No. That's ridiculous. I gave him some advice regarding his beagle when I ran into him at the Piggly Wiggly yesterday." She scoffed at Nolie's words. "What's going on? I've been in this town for seven years and no one's shown an interest."

"That's because you looked like a pubescent teen."

"Excuse me?"

"I heard you wore a dress to that small-business meeting last night," Nolie said.

"Who told you that?"

"I have my sources." She offered Jena a copy of the day's schedule and the phone messages. "By the way, you look very nice."

"Thank you," Jena mumbled. She reviewed the papers and looked up. "What's this?"

"Rebel Photography called. They can get Ernie in after lunch next Saturday."

Jena brightened. "Really? That's wonderful." Her plan to make Ernie the face of the Jingle Paws event was actually moving forward and none too soon.

"Pilar said she'd give Ernie a bath before you go. We want her to look her best so she'll make lots of money for the rescue."

"Yes. Yes, thank you."

"Oh, and I have good news. I called Dee Smith yesterday afternoon and sent her for a physical."

"Everything checked out?"

"Glowing references. Everyone loves her. And the electronic background check came back clean."

"Wonderful." Jena couldn't help a smile as she realized things were beginning to look up, especially compared to last week.

"Yes, I agree," Nolie added. "Maybe we can cross train her to answer the phones, too."

"Great idea." Jena paused. "I think Dee can handle that. She seems very mature for her age."

"That's the truth. A lot more mature than my kids were at eighteen." Nolie looked at Jena. "What were you like as a teenager, Dr. Harper?"

"Naive and foolish." *I made mistakes that have haunted me my entire life*, Jena silently added. Mistakes that left her wondering every single day about the daughter she gave up.

"I find that hard to believe," Nolie said, dismissing the notion. She removed the rubber band from *The Weekly Rebel* and spread the paper out on the counter. "Will you look at this?" She pointed to the front page. "Dr. Rainbolt."

Jena leaned closer. There it was, above the fold. A shot of Tucker and Chester. The photo had been snapped the moment she'd handed off the kitten. In the background, the citizens gazed at Tucker with adoration in their eyes. And where was she? Still in the tree.

Tucker was always going to be a superhero to the people of Rebel. She didn't want the spotlight, but she did want to at least be listed in the credits. The only way that would happen would be if she continued to step up her game.

"Good picture," Jena admitted as she headed to the waiting room closet with her coat. "I imagine it will sell a lot of papers."

"Oh, and Dr. Harper, have you decided what our holiday hours will be? I need to shore up my travel plans to visit my children."

Normally, she and Tucker worked on the holiday schedule together, but there was no point waiting for him. "On my to-do list," Jena said. "It will be up by the end of the day."

The front door opened and Dee walked in, along with a draft of chilly air. Today, her hair had been pulled into a pert ponytail at the back of her head and she wore white faux fur earmuffs. She grinned and gave Jena a wave as she tugged off her coat.

"Glad to see you." Jena smiled. She took Dee's coat and hung it next to hers. "I prayed that you wouldn't decide to follow the help wanted sign in the Eagle Donuts shop window and never return."

"They're hiring, too?"

"Yes, but their only employee benefit is free donuts. Who needs free éclairs when you can have free kittens at Rebel Vet and Rescue?"

"Welcome to the team, Dee," Nolie said.

"Thank you." Dee pulled off her earmuffs and tucked them in her tote bag.

"Now that we work together, do you think I could have the recipe for those amazing brownies?" Nolie asked.

A bright smile filled Dee's face. "You liked them?"

"My mouth gave them a solid ten and my hips agreed," Nolie returned.

Dee laughed. "Sure. I'm happy to share."

Jena nodded toward her office. "Follow me." She led her around the reception desk and down the hall. "This is my private office. Private, because it has a door. Other than that, it resembles a closet."

Dee glanced around.

"Impressive, right?" Jena's gaze swept the old desk and chair and the ancient bookshelves crammed into the tiny space.

"Since I've never had my own office, yes. Very impressive."

"I'm half of Rebel Vet and Rescue. You met Dr. Rainbolt on Saturday."

"Yes. Mrs. Parker said his patients' owners call him Dr. Blue-Eyes behind his back." Dee smiled.

Jena laughed. "Yes, and Dr. Blue-Eyes is only in this clinic half-days on Monday, Wednesday and Friday, normally. We alternate Saturdays unless we're slammed. The rest of the time he's at the equine clinic at Rebel Ranch." She shrugged. "Wherever he is, his fans follow. Dr. Rainbolt is good for business."

As Jena recited the schedule, the stark reality that soon she would be the only vet in the clinic the six days a week they were open hit home for the second time that morning with grim clarity.

"Oklahoma State." Dee inspected Jena's framed diploma on the wall near the door, a musing smile on her face.

"You mentioned OSU, too. What sort of major were you looking at?"

"I really didn't have a clue. Another reason not to spend money that I don't have." She moved around the room, examining patient photos on the walls with interest and asking questions. "I love animals," Dee murmured.

"How much?" Jena pushed the stack of papers on her desk aside and perched on the corner.

"Excuse me?"

"I asked how much you love animals."

"We have a cat and two dogs at home."

"What are your thoughts on litter boxes?"

This time it was Dee who laughed. "I haven't thought about them lately."

"Well, do. This job is all guts and little glory."

"What does that mean?"

"It means these animals are everything to me, but the job can be messy, unpleasant and sometimes even sad."

"I've got a lot of experience with all three."

Jena's gaze was pulled to Dee's brown eyes. They were absolutely without guile, and in that moment, it became clear that she and Dee had a lot in common. They'd walked the same path at some point.

"I need help in the clinic and the rescue," Jena said. "You'll train with Pilar Lopez. She's a certified tech. More than that, she loves the animals, and she's good at what she does. You can learn a lot from her, maybe even get certified yourself someday."

Dee nodded. "Thank you for the opportunity."

Jena opened the closet that was crowded with supplies, and reached for a large cardboard box. "How tall are you?"

"Five-four."

"So am I." Jena opened the flaps of the box and pulled out plastic packages that held navy scrubs. "This is your uniform. The first two pairs are free. You can buy another set at the local Budget-Mart."

"Scrubs." Dee reached for the folded packages and held them to her chest, her eyes beaming with pride.

It was years ago, but Jena remembered her first pair of real scrubs. The moment she donned them as a volunteer at a rescue in Tulsa, she had known that she wanted to take care of animals for the rest of her life. Shortly after that revelation, her life had gone off course, but her love of animals never did.

"You're really hiring me?" Dee asked. Her eyes brightened and she grinned.

"Yes. Your background check came back clear. If you still need a place to stay, there's a studio apartment over the rescue. Any interest?"

"I'm very interested."

Jena quoted the financial information as she opened the desk drawer and pulled out the keys. "Do you want to take a look?"

"I don't need to look. I'll take it. There's nothing available in Rebel right now that's within my budget. I've been staying with a girlfriend in Tulsa."

"Great. Water and electric are included in the rent. It's furnished, though nothing spectacular. The entrance is around the corner at Oak and Second Street."

"No deposit or anything?"

"We do things very casually in small towns. Besides, I know where you work. A handshake will suffice." Jena held out the keys, which were attached to a Rebel Clinic logo key chain and then offered her hand.

Dee took them and then grasped Jena's hand, visibly moved with emotion. "Thank you." The young woman's voice trembled as she said the words. "I won't let you down, Dr. Harper."

"I know you won't," Jena murmured, touched by Dee's heartfelt response.

Silence stretched for a moment before Dee

cleared her throat and stared at the keys with reverence.

"Is this your first apartment?" Jena asked.

Dee nodded, excitement dancing in her brown eyes.

"Ah, then this is a big milestone." Jena smiled. "Do you have family around here, Dee?"

"Only my dad. He's in Tulsa. My mother passed a year ago." She bit her lip and stared at the ground as she said the words.

Jena's chest ached for the young woman. "Oh, Dee, I'm so sorry for your loss. You're an only child?"

Dee nodded.

"So am I. You're welcome to invite your dad to come by and see the clinic. We'd love to meet him."

"Um… Well, remember I said things were complicated?"

"Yes."

"He's not happy with me right now. I know he means well, but his plans for my life aren't my plans." Dee looked at Jena and stared at her for a moment as if searching for an answer. "Sometimes you have to do what you know in your gut is the right thing. Don't you think?"

"I do," Jena returned without hesitation. She understood that sentiment only too well. Eighteen years ago it meant having her baby, and resulted in losing everything when her family turned their backs on her because of her decision. She absolutely knew she had done the right thing then.

Though Dee's family problems really weren't any of her business, Jena couldn't stop the words that slipped from her lips. "If you ever need to talk, my door is open."

"Thank you. I appreciate that." Dee smiled and turned away. Then she stopped, looking back. "Chester. Did you find a home for him yet?"

"We did not. He'll have his neuter surgery soon and by the time the adoption event is here, he'll be ready for you to fill out the paperwork and take him home."

"Oh, thank you!"

When Dee smiled, staring at her with so much trust, the funny feeling of connection washed over Jena again. It was like a familiar song whose words she couldn't quite place.

Her gaze followed Dee and her bobbing blue ponytail as she left the room, and then Jena slowly shook her head.

"What's going on here, Lord?" Jena murmured.

Whatever it was, she'd like to be let in on the secret. Soon.

Chapter Four

"Nolie, what are all these boxes?" Tucker dodged a hanging turkey, probably the brother of the one who'd attacked him last week, and inched around the boxes in the break room. He counted at least ten of them.

"The small ones are promotional pens, and I'm pretty sure the other boxes are Rebel Vet and Rescue logo tumblers with straws." Nolie inspected the packing slip on the largest box. "Dr. Harper was very careful to order the BPA-free kind."

"Why?"

"Because they're safe for our customers."

"No. Why did Dr. Harper order all of this?"

She looked at him like he'd grown another head. "For Jingle Paws."

"Jingle Paws. Right." Tucker nodded as though that made complete sense.

It had only been a week since she first mentioned the idea. Yet, Jena was full steam ahead without him on the project, while Tucker was still trying to get a handle on the change of attitude of his best friend. He glanced at the boxes again. Where did she get the funds for all this swag?

He reached for the coffee carafe. "When is Jingle Paws?"

"The second weekend in December," Nolie said. "That's only four weeks away. Lots to do." She cleared her throat. "For all of us."

Tucker got the message loud and clear. He might have done his part if Jena had kept him in the loop. He glanced at the calendar on the wall.

Four weeks until Jingle Paws and then three weeks until he left. Who was he kidding? He'd been so busy talking to a real estate agent in Texas and preparing for the Texas State Veterinary Licensing Exam, that lately, he barely knew what day it was.

After adding cream to his mug, Tucker leaned against the wall. "So where is everybody?"

"We're closed the rest of the day. The adoption event starts at noon."

"Right. Right. Where's Dr. Harper? I saw her car outside."

"She and Ernie walked down to the photography studio. They're having photos done for the Jingle Paws posters. Ernie's the poster pet for the event."

"Got it," he said. But once again, he didn't. In fact, the more they chatted, the more he realized how out of touch he was with his own clinic. "How's the new hire coming along?"

"She's great. Pilar is training her."

"Glad to hear that. I talked to her on Friday when the pizzas arrived. She likes anchovies, too. That doesn't bode well for my pineapple." He paused. "Her name is Dee, right?"

"That's right."

"She remind you of anyone?"

"The pastor's mama is the only other person I know with blue hair, and she's eighty-six, so that would be a no."

"I'm probably imagining things." Or was he? Sometimes when Dee frowned she looked exactly like Jena, and it caught him off guard. Yesterday he even heard Dee laugh and turned around, thinking it was Jena. How strange was that? And why was he the only person who noticed? Maybe he just had Jena on his mind. Yeah, that might explain it.

He was spending way too much time processing how Jena had changed since the co-op meeting. And it wasn't just her appearance. She was confident and bossy. Real bossy.

Nolie narrowed her gaze. "Everything okay in your world, Doc?"

"Huh?" He looked up. "What?"

"I asked if everything was all right. You seem a little distracted." She slid a pen behind her ear and stared at him. "You sure have had a lot of phone calls since you got back from your trip, too. Are the girls okay? Anything I can do to help?"

"Nothing to report. Just busy." He took a long swallow of coffee. They were going to have to tell the staff what was going on soon. Hopefully, Jena had a plan for that, too. "My next appointment isn't until three p.m. I think I'll head down to Rebel Photography to check out the photo shoot." He paused. "Nolie, could you call the lab and get the test results on the dachshund that I saw late yesterday?"

"Yes, sir. I can do that."

Tucker pulled his Stetson and lined denim jacket out of the closet, then headed down Main Street. As he walked, a few locals waved, offering comments about his picture in *The Weekly Rebel*. The paper came out last week and he still hadn't seen it yet. Tucker made a mental note to ask Nolie where the clinic's copy was.

When he pulled open the door of Rebel Photography, Ernie barked, greeting him with enthusiasm. "Ernie. How's my girl?"

Jena looked up and her eyes widened. "Tucker. I didn't expect to see you here."

"Just thought I'd offer my support." He took the seat next to Jena and scratched Ernie behind the ears. The pup blissfully leaned against his leg.

"That's really nice of you." Jena stared at him almost like Nolie had. Was it that unbelievable that he'd lend support to a friend? Then it occurred to him that he had been wrapped up in his own life for the last…four years. But hey, he had kids. He was a single father. A business owner.

A guy lost in a fog was more like it. A fog that was only just starting to clear. Tucker frowned. Had he deluded himself into thinking he'd been there for Jena all these years?

"Were we in the newspaper?" he asked.

"You were on the front page of *The Weekly Rebel* with Chester last week."

"That's wrong. You did all the work."

"But you're the face of the clinic."

"Cut that out. We're both the face of the clinic." He looked around the room. "Where is everyone?"

"In back. We're next," Jena said. "They've got a couple in there for an anniversary photo session. Sixty-five years. Can you believe that?"

"That's a long time," he said. "I don't know anyone with that kind of track record. Do you?"

"I don't have much of a family tree, but my great-aunt's marriage lasted for over forty years until my great-uncle passed."

"Forty years is pretty impressive. You know my family tree is sparse, too." She was one of the few people who got that.

Tucker rarely talked about his parents. His mother had passed when he was a kid and his father ran off. He'd been raised by his brother Mitch. Not much to talk about, except that he owed both of his big brothers everything, a fact which made it increasingly difficult to leave Rebel and disappoint them.

"Maybe the Rainbolts are writing a new chapter," Jena said.

"What?" He looked at her.

"Well, Mitch and Reece are both married now. Happily ever after might be your new family motto."

Tucker chuckled. "And you accuse me of being the optimistic one?"

"I'm talking Rainbolts here. As for myself, I think we know that I'm not likely to find any sort of HEA."

"Don't say that. You deserve to find love, same as anyone else. More, maybe. You're a giving person."

"Why, Tucker, thank you." Her mouth quivered with emotion.

"It's true." Jena was the nicest and most generous person he knew, and he did want the best for her. Only as he sat there looking at her, with her cute pixie haircut and those big brown eyes, it occurred to him that the idea of some slacker like Mike from Beep Jeep winning her over had him getting crankier by the minute.

Both Tucker and Jena turned when an elderly woman and her husband came out of the back room. The woman paused to pet Ernie. She offered Jena and Tucker a generous smile. "Oh, look at you two with your dog. How sweet. How long have you been married?"

"Us?" Tucker sputtered. He choked out an awkward laugh. "No. We're not." He waved a hand between them.

"We're friends," Jena quickly added. "Best friends. We work together. Rebel Vet and Rescue," Jena added. "Down on the corner."

The woman nodded, still smiling, as if she knew something they didn't. "My husband is my best friend, too."

Tucker opened his mouth and closed it, not daring to look at Jena. Normally, he'd be able to laugh something like this off. Today, that wasn't working and he wasn't sure why.

They were both silent as the elderly couple left the studio.

"Dr. Rainbolt. I didn't realize you were going to be here, too."

Tucker looked up and then stood when the photographer entered the waiting area. "Morning, ma'am." *JoJo.* Her pet's name came unbidden to his mind. Too bad he couldn't remember the woman's name. He smiled and shoved his hands into his pockets.

"Oh, you're very photogenic." She walked around him, assessing him from all angles. "Yes. Very nice."

Tucker coughed. "I'm just here for support."

"Still, let's get you and Ernie on film and see if I'm right."

Uncomfortable upstaging Jena, he turned to her. "That's not what you had in mind, is it? I mean, this is your project, right?"

Jena turned to the photographer. "Could you give us a few minutes to discuss this, Jane?"

"Of course."

"Jane," Tucker said. "That's her name."

"Cocker spaniel," they both said at the same time.

"Right," Jena said. "Now about the session."

"I'm not here to horn in on your project, Jena."

She shrugged. "The way I see it is that if Ernie can sell tickets, then you and Ernie can sell twice as many. I'm not about to let my ego stand in the way of what will benefit the rescue. If you're okay with being exploited for your good looks, I am, too."

"My good looks?" He blinked at her words.

"Come on, Tuck. You aren't blind. Surely you know what they call you, right?"

"No, actually, I don't. And who is this 'they'?"

"Our patients' owners. And they call you Dr. Blue-Eyes."

He blinked again. This was news to him. "I'm being objectified at the clinic?"

"It's not your fault you're handsome, but there it is."

"You think I'm handsome, too?" Unless he

was hallucinating, Jena just called him hand-some. Like, twice.

Jena's face pinked. "It's a fact. Not an opinion. It just is."

"Interesting." He grinned, oddly buoyed by the conversation. "I'll do it if it will help you, Jena."

She looked away. "As I said, I feel confident it will help the rescue, so you'd be helping more than me."

"I'm willing to sacrifice for the greater good."

"That's very altruistic of you."

"I thought so, too," he said, trying to suppress a grin.

The photo shoot took a lot longer than Tucker expected. Jane was really into the whole Christmas theme. She played holiday music, brought out a box filled with Christmas accessories and tried every item on him and Ernie. At one point there was even a dusting of faux snow. After forty-five minutes of being positioned and repositioned and filmed from every unbelievable angle, Ernie stretched and then whined and walked in circles. Tucker heartily agreed.

"Ernie wants to go out." Tucker nodded toward the back door. "How about if the pup and I go for a walk, while you two review those three thousand pictures that Jane took?"

"Thanks, Tucker," Jena said.

He pulled the reindeer antlers off of Ernie and led her outside.

Fifteen minutes later, Tucker slipped in the back door in time to hear Jena speaking.

"What do you think, Jane?"

"I think these are amazing shots. Your boss should have been a model."

"He's not my boss," Jena returned flatly. "But yes, Tucker was born that way. He can't help it."

"And you get to work with him?"

"It's a cross I bear."

"I wouldn't mind. What's it like to work with Tucker Rainbolt? All the Rainbolt men are handsome, but Tucker has that extra boyish quality going for him."

"Boyish? Please," Jena scoffed. "He's just an ordinary guy. Annoying, stubborn, totally clueless."

Tucker jerked back at the words, mystified by the exchange, and not sure if he'd been complimented or insulted.

"Still…" Jane continued.

"You're married." Jena admonished.

"Maybe so, but I'm also an artist and I can well appreciate God's handiwork."

"Nice try, but you were ogling my best friend."

"No, that was professional appreciation."

Ernie barked when Jena burst out in a full-on belly laugh.

"So are Ernie and I done?" Tucker asked as he stepped into the room.

Jena whirled around, her face pink and her eyes guilty. "I think so. Right, Jane?"

"Yes," Jane returned, without looking at him. "We have plenty of options here."

"Great." He turned to Jena. "Are you and Ernie headed back to the clinic?"

"Yes. Pilar and I will be loading the kennels into the clinic van."

"Do you want help?"

"No, but thank you. We've got Dee helping, as well. I just need you to be your charming self and convince people that they need a furry animal to make their life complete." She looked up at him. "Are you bringing the girls?"

"Yeah. I'm going to go get them shortly. They're excited." He paused, trying to find a way to segue into another topic. "I hoped we could talk about Jingle Paws."

"What is there to talk about?" Her short legs pumped faster to keep up with Ernie's tongue-lolling enthusiastic stride.

Tucker sped up, too. "Shouldn't we sit down and look at the budget before you spend clinic funds on the rescue fundraiser?"

Jena stopped on the sidewalk, and he nearly ran into her. She crossed her arms and stared at him. Ernie looked at both of them and whined. "What are you talking about?" she asked.

"The pens and tumblers? The photographer?"

She released a slow breath. "Tucker, Jingle

Paws is my project, and sponsors donated the funds for those promotional items. I did not dip into the clinic budget. As for the photographer, she also donated her services as an event sponsor. Official sponsors will have their names and web addresses go on the tote bags and the swag that attendees will receive."

"Sponsor?" Uh-oh. He swallowed.

"Yes. What part of that do you object to?"

"None, and I apologize for jumping to conclusions." He stepped carefully to his next thought. "But maybe I could review your plans for Jingle Paws. I might be able to help."

"This is my project. I won't be taking funds from the clinic or the rescue budget to launch Jingle Paws, so you don't need to worry." She started walking again. "Come on, Ernie, let's go."

Tucker followed her. "I wasn't exactly worried. I thought I could contribute."

"You just did," she said. "You and Ernie are now the face of Jingle Paws. I have everything else under control."

He opened his mouth and then closed it. Jena was right. He'd delivered an impossible challenge two weeks ago and, while he was making plans to leave town, she'd been putting a solution into action.

"You know what?" he said. "I'm going to pull my foot out of my mouth right now. I was wrong and I'm really sorry." He turned on his heel, willing to retreat before he did any further damage.

"Where are you going?" Jena asked.

"I need a few things at the Piggly Wiggly, then I'll pick up the girls for the adoption event." He nodded. "See you there."

When Tucker entered the little grocery store, he nearly ran into Mike Ross. Just what he needed after aggravating his best friend.

"Hey, Tucker, have you seen Jena?" The other man was all used-car salesman smiles.

"Are you stalking her now?"

"No. I'm helping her with Jingle Bells. Surely she mentioned that."

"It's Jingle Paws."

"Whatever."

Tucker clenched his jaw. So, Ross got to help, but he didn't. Where was the logic there? "You don't have a phone?" he asked.

"She's not picking up." He shrugged. "I saw her walking down Main Street. Thought maybe she ducked in here."

Tucker scowled, inordinately annoyed, for reasons he couldn't pinpoint at the moment. "Come on Ross, what's the deal? Why the sudden interest in Jena?"

"The deal is that Jena is a very attractive woman. It was an oversight on my part not to have noticed it before." He looked Tucker up and down. "Frankly, I'm a little surprised you haven't made a move on her. But I guess that's your loss."

Tucker gave a slow nod as he tamped down the rising swell of irritation. He pointed toward First Street, the opposite direction of the clinic. "I think she headed that way."

"Thanks, bro. I appreciate it."

"Bro," Tucker grumbled with distaste. He didn't need another bro in his life right now. What he needed was to figure out how to support Jena without stepping on her toes.

"We put ads in all the local area papers, so hopefully we'll have a good turnout," Jena said to Dee. Holding a clipboard in one hand and a tote bag in the other, she surveyed the community center's main lobby. Visitors were already popping in to see the cute kenneled rescue animals.

"You look really nice, Dr. Harper," Dee said.

"Um, thank you."

Jena had desperately wanted to wear jeans and a volunteer T-shirt. Being comfortable might help with her nerves, but she'd resisted the urge. *I'm the boss now.* She'd quoted the mantra and changed into a skirt and sweater with ballerina flats. She'd gone the distance and worn a freshly starched lab coat, too.

"Could I follow you around for a little while? I mean, since this is my first adoption event," Dee said.

"Of course, then you'll want to observe the volunteers. They make the event," Jena said. "The volunteers answer questions and handle the one-on-ones with customers and pets to ensure a better adoption experience for the attendees and our animals."

"So people just pick out an animal and leave with them?"

"It's not quite that simple. We have classrooms in the center reserved to allow prospective adoptive parents to spend a little time with an animal, to determine if they're a good fit. That's really encouraged. Plus, everyone must fill out a very detailed application. We do waive the adoption fees today. The important thing is that all adoptive parents understand that they can bring the animal back to the clinic if it doesn't work out."

Dee nodded as she listened.

"We've got the Jingle Paws event coming up and that will see more adoptions, so I'm not concerned about numbers today."

"I'd love to volunteer in the rescue."

"Pilar will have you in the rescue after you're trained in the clinic. Then when you feel comfortable, we'll have you working directly with the public, too."

"I can't wait." She glanced around. "Look. There's Dr. Rainbolt. I didn't know that he has children."

"Hmm?" Jena looked up in response to the sudden change in topic.

"Aunty Jena!"

Hazel and Ginger skipped toward her in matching corduroy jumpers over sweaters and leggings.

Jena's heart caught at the sight of her precious godchildren. She knelt down and threw her arms open wide. "My girls are here."

Once again, they called her name in unison, stretching their arms and begging to be hugged. She obliged, giving each a noisy, tickling kiss on the nose and on the ears. Then she examined the abrasion on Ginger's chin and offered the brave four-year-old an extra kiss.

"Daddy says this is from my first flying lesson."

"You're much too young for flying," Jena said, clucking her tongue. "Let's walk from now on, baby girl."

Tucker strolled behind them, hands in his pockets, wearing a crisp lab coat with a stethoscope around his neck and looking handsome as usual, which would benefit the adoption event. Everyone wanted Dr. Blue-Eyes as their pet's veterinarian.

Jena offered him a cool nod of greeting and kept her gaze on the little munchkins. It was difficult to remain annoyed at Tucker when he brought her favorite little people to see her, but she wasn't ready to let him off the hook that easily. It was clear from earlier today that he doubted that she could run Jingle Paws without him. Well, how did he think she would manage the clinic when he was gone?

"They look adorable. Who dressed them?" she asked.

"Mrs. Stewart. If it was me, I would have let them convince me it was okay to come in their footed pajamas. Their nanny is no pushover."

"We all need a Mrs. Stewart in our life."

"Do we?" Tucker asked. "Who's yours?"

"Nolie, of course."

"I can see that." Tucker glanced around the community center and offered a slow nod. "Nice turnout, huh?"

"That picture of you in *The Weekly Rebel* didn't hurt things. The rescue has had a deluge of requests for cats and kittens."

"I suspect Chester is the real lure," Tucker said.

Jena shook her head. She'd stand by her claim that the man was clueless. Chester was cute but the women of Rebel were dreaming of Dr. Blue-Eyes to go along with their furry pets. She wouldn't be a bit surprised if appointments requesting Dr. Rainbolt increased soon, as well.

As if on cue, Hazel and Ginger's attention moved quickly from Aunty Jena to the kennel where little Chester sat looking absolutely adorable, licking his paws and cleaning his coat.

"Daddy, may we have another cat?" Ginger asked.

"Not today," Tucker said. "But we can help find them homes."

"The center opened their concession stand for us today," Jena said. "Mind if I take the girls for a juice?"

"Sure," Tucker said. "I'll take a walk around and see how I can encourage a few adoptions."

"That would be much appreciated," Jena said. "I'm hoping we can get a few more into homes before Jingle Paws."

"You can count on me, Boss," he said.

She offered him a humorless stare as he turned and walked away. Her mistake had been spending so many years as his comic side-kick. Getting him to take her seriously after seven years wasn't going to be easy.

"Cookies?" Hazel asked Jena.

"How about a yummy banana?"

The girls looked at each other and then nodded.

When they were settled at a table with their juice and slices of banana, Jena pulled two books out of her tote bag. "I brought you presents."

"Nice tote bag," Dee said.

Jena glanced up at Dee and then at her baby blue-and-white striped bag. "Eagle Donuts provides these for our adoptive parents. We throw in the animal's favorite toys and their favorite food, along with a coupon for a discount on their first visit to the clinic. You'll get one when you take Chester home."

"A bag and a furr-ever baby. I like that," Dee said.

While the twins turned the pages of the books and chatted between themselves, Jena and Dee drank coffee.

"They're so sweet," Dee said. "So Dr. Rainbolt is married?"

"He's widowed," Jena said the words softly.

"And you and Dr. Rainbolt? You're...like, dating?"

Jena nearly dropped her lidded cup of coffee. "Dating?" She lowered her voice again. "No. Why would you think that?"

"I don't know. I've only been here a short time, but it's obvious that he's really fond of you, and he watches you a lot. I noticed it Friday, during our staff meeting."

"No. We've been friends a long time. That's all."

Dee only raised her brows.

"Really. We're just friends." Jena rolled Dee's observation over in her mind. Ridiculous. Tucker thought of her as his annoying best friend. That was all.

"So who are you dating?" Dee asked.

"Are we supposed to discuss my dating life? I'm your boss."

"We could discuss mine, except I haven't met anyone since I moved to Rebel."

"Things get better during tourist season. The population explodes when it's warm and city people head out to Rebel Lake and Keystone Lake. Right now, the majority of the good citizens of Rebel are, um…mature. Very mature. Which is not a bad thing."

"Unless you aren't."

Jena laughed. "That is very true."

"I think I'll go start my adoption paperwork for Chester," Dee said. "Will you be okay here?"

"Me? Of course, these girls are like my own."

Dee started to leave and then hesitated. "Have you ever thought about having children, Dr. Harper?"

"Thought about it? Yes. But I try not to dwell on the fact that it's probably never going to happen." Jena silently amended the sentence. *Never again in this lifetime.*

"There you two are! I've been looking for you."

Both Jena and Dee turned. "Is there a problem, Nolie?" Jena asked.

"Officer Gallegos is looking for you, Dr. Harper." Nolie turned to Dee. "And Pilar needs your help to take the dogs outside for their restroom breaks."

"Nolie, can you stay with the twins?" Jena asked.

"Of course, I can. They're simply adorable." A sigh slipped from her lips and she shook her head. "Why my children won't give me twins, I don't know."

"You know it doesn't work like that, right?" Jena asked.

"Go," Nolie said with a wave of her fingers. "Officer Gallegos awaits. He's near the front entrance." She offered one of her all too familiar know-it-all smiles.

So the Rebel Police Department deputy had tracked her down. Jena was surprised to see him out of uniform. In jeans and a leather jacket, he stood looking over the activities with a smile on his face.

"Officer Gallegos," Jena said.

He swung around and smiled, giving her appearance an appreciative but respectful glance. Officer Gallegos was a nice-looking man. Just not her type. If she had a type.

"You can call me Ramon, Doc. I'm off duty."

"How can I help you… Ramon?"

"I want to offer my services."

Jena tensed and raised her brows.

"I'd like to volunteer for Jingle Paws."

"Oh. Wonderful. How did you find out about it?"

"My sister runs Rebel Curls."

"Oh, that new hair place on Rebel Avenue, across from the pharmacy."

"That's it. She was at the co-op meeting and heard you speak and suggested I contact you."

"You want to volunteer? That's why you've

been looking for me?" Jena released a breath of relief.

"Well, that's not quite all, to be honest." He looked at the floor, and then slowly met her gaze. "I'm a single dad and my son is in scouts with Pilar Lopez's son. She works for you."

"Yes. I know." Jena bit back a smile as she began to understand the direction that the conversation was headed. Pilar wasn't just her best employee, she was also a single mom with a sweet little boy.

"I'm sort of, well, I get tongue-tied talking to women."

"You're talking to me."

"That's different."

This time Jena did smile. It was different because he didn't have a crush on her.

"I'm pretty sure Pilar doesn't dislike me." He swallowed. "I thought that maybe if she got to know me, without the uniform…well, who knows? She might say yes to coffee or an outing with our boys."

"Ah," Jena murmured with a nod. "I think I can help you."

"You can?"

"Absolutely. Our website has a sign-up form for Jingle Paw volunteers. Sign up and we'll send you a schedule. I wouldn't be surprised if you were scheduled to volunteer at the same time as people you know." She raised her brows. "If you get my drift."

He grinned. "Thanks, Doc. I really appreciate this."

"I appreciate you volunteering."

Jena clutched the clipboard to her chest and smiled as Ramon Gallegos walked away.

"You look pleased with yourself."

She turned at Tucker's voice, still basking in warm fuzzies at the thought of connecting sweet Pilar with Officer Gallegos. "I guess I am."

He frowned. "Nolie says you have a suitor?"

"Nolie is wrong. Officer Gallegos volunteered for Jingle Paws and he also mentioned he has a crush on Pilar. I'm going to help things along."

"You're matchmaking on the side?"

"It's a free service, and it's a secret," she said. "Although, if I end up losing the clinic and the rescue it could be my next career, I suppose."

"Don't even say that. You are not going to lose anything." He hesitated. "And look, about earlier, my comments about the Jingle Paws swag and all. I really am sorry. I was out of line. My only defense is that I felt like you were shutting me out."

"No," she said the word slowly. "I'm simply practicing being on my own."

"Yeah, I figured that out once I stopped thinking everything was about me. You're doing a great job, Jena."

"Thank you," she said, pleased at the admission. Being at odds with Tucker only made her heart ache and added to the other dozen reasons she couldn't sleep at night.

"I think we need to talk to the staff, Jena. They need to know."

"Yes, you're right." She couldn't help but sigh, dreading the prospect. "Nolie already suspects something is up. How about pizza day?"

"The Friday before the week of Thanksgiving? You don't think maybe we should do it sooner? Like, Monday? Let them get used to the idea."

"Think about it, Tucker. We're always swamped right before the Thanksgiving holiday because we're closed Wednesday afternoon through Saturday the following week. I can't handle a full caseload and Nolie's drama."

"Yeah. Okay, I get that. Friday it is."

"Wow." She blinked as she realized that it was less than two weeks until Thanksgiving.

"What?"

"Time is slipping away."

"Tell me about it. I haven't had a single inquiry about the equine clinic, either," Tucker said.

"We expected that. You can always refer your patients to the Hominy practice."

"If I have to, or maybe I'm not supposed to go to Texas."

Jena whirled around and looked at him. If Tucker needed an attitude adjustment, well so did she. There was no way she wanted to hold back her best friend. "Don't say that," she said. "This is a great opportunity for you. It's what you want. Don't let the details here hold you back."

"You want me to go?"

"I want you to be happy, Tucker. In the end, that's what we both want for each other. Everything here will fall into place, somehow."

"It's really strange how you're starting to sound more and more like me. I'm not sure if that's a good thing." He cocked his head and stared at Jena, really stared, like he was fighting an internal battle. "You've changed, Jena."

"I should hope so."

He didn't comment, though it seemed that he wanted to.

"I've got to check on the volunteers," she said.

"Wait." Tucker placed a hand on her arm, and she froze at the contact. "I'm taking the girls to the Arrowhead Diner after the event. Would you join us?" His gaze was sincere and searching as his eyes met hers.

"Breakfast for dinner?" Jena perked up. It was a ritual on adoption event day. They'd been doing it for years, but she hadn't even considered it this time. Tucker had been so busy lately.

"What do you say?" he persisted.

"You're on. Besides, I have to get as much twin time in as I can before you leave."

"What about best friend time?" he asked.

"That, too," Jena murmured.

Yes, chicken and waffles at the Arrowhead Diner for the last time and maybe she'd be able to pretend everything was normal for a little while longer.

Chapter Five

❦

"Your mare looks good. The ultrasound and fetal heartbeat are all normal." Tucker removed the examination sleeve from his arm and turned to his brother Reece. "Junior is right on target to peek his head into the world near the end of foaling season."

"Junior will be my daughter's horse," Reece said.

"Your daughter." Tucker grinned and shook his head. "Who would have thought? Reece Rainbolt, family man."

"I don't deserve half of the blessings the good Lord has given me this year."

The expression of humility and gratitude on his big brother's face caused Tucker to pause. "We all have lots to be thankful for this year," he finally said.

"I agree. And that reminds me. Did you invite Jena to Thanksgiving dinner?" Reece asked.

Tucker grimaced. "I put it on my Monday to-do list just this morning."

"And promptly forgot. Right?"

"I can neither confirm nor deny." He soaped up his hands and arms in the stable sink. Jena always turned down his invites to Rainbolt events and he knew he'd have to really put on a hard sell to convince her that she wasn't intruding.

"You forgot."

"Where is Thanksgiving dinner anyhow?" Tucker asked, once again bypassing the question. "Haven't we outgrown everyone's house?"

"Not my house," Reece said.

That was the truth. Tucker's second oldest brother lived in a ridiculously large house a stone's throw up the road from Tucker's own home. Reece shared the place with his new wife, their daughter and several animals.

"The newlyweds are hosting?"

"Daisy and Mitch don't have enough room. Are you volunteering?"

"Me? What are you talking about? Daisy and Mitch's kids alone would fill my house." Tucker reached for a paper towel. "I think the important question here is will Luna be cooking?"

"No, Luna is not cooking. She has her own family." Reece stared at his little brother. "Are you insulting my wife's culinary skills?"

Tucker raised his hands. "Not at all. It was just a question."

"Claire plans to prepare two birds along with the fixings. Daisy is bringing pies from her bakery."

"What should I bring?" Tucker asked. With his schedule of late, he contemplated whether a couple bags of chips and some dip would be acceptable.

"I don't know. Call Claire and ask her," Reece grumbled. "This whole thing is stressing me out. You know it's a lot of responsibility having your family over for dinner."

"Didn't mean to stress you." He hesitated. "What are you making?"

"I'm in charge of rounding up my family," Reece returned.

"That doesn't seem to be an equitable distribution of dinner assignments."

"Excuse me? Sure it is. I have to go to Tulsa and buy a bigger table for the dining room. That's my contribution."

Tucker did a mental head count of the Rainbolt family. "We're up to somewhere around sixteen, aren't we?"

"Yeah, it's out of control."

"Next Thursday, right?"

Reece gave an exasperated sigh as he rolled his eyes. "Seriously, Tuck? Thanksgiving is always on a Thursday. Are you messing with me?"

"I'm verifying. What's wrong with that?"

His brother stared at him. "You tell me."

"Hey, I've got a lot going on right now." A total understatement. Not only did he have the future to plan and prepare for, but saying goodbye to Rebel weighed heavily on his heart.

"You're moving to Texas. I get that." Reece frowned. "What else is going on?"

"I'm studying for the Texas vet exam on top of everything else." He sighed. "Turns out they like their vets licensed."

"You'll be teaching, not practicing, college boy."

"A license is required. Besides, the plan is to put in some hours with a local practice to keep my skills sharp."

"Oh, now I get it. You have a back-up plan." Reece gave a knowing nod.

"What's that supposed to mean?"

"It means that if you don't like it you can hit the escape button and go back to doing what you were born to do."

"No. That's not it at all." Yet as he said the words, Tucker wondered if Reece was right. Was he giving himself a safety net? Had his second thoughts, his doubts, begun to overshadow his plans?

"Anyhow, quit changing the subject," Reece said. "Are you going to invite Jena to Thanksgiving dinner or not?"

Tucker pulled the stethoscope from around his neck and grabbed his medical bag. "I don't know.

Jena is skittish about what she calls horning in on family events."

"She came to the family gathering at Daisy's last summer," Reece said.

"That was different."

Different because she hadn't just overheard himself and Reece talk about her. Different because she hadn't been humiliated.

Tucker thought back to Saturday dinner with Jena and his girls at the Arrowhead Diner. It had been a fun time. She had been in good spirits when they parted, and he was reluctant to risk upsetting her again.

"Different how? What's going on?" his brother persisted. "Is she mad at you?"

"No, she's not exactly mad." He started out of the stables with his brother right behind. "The thing is, Jena overheard my conversation with you about buying the building."

"Oh, man," Reece said. "That's not good. You sure messed that up."

"Me?"

"Yeah, you."

Tucker tugged on the brim of his hat. Reece was right. He'd swooped in and attempted to handle the building situation without even discussing things with Jena.

"Okay, yeah. I messed up," he finally said. "So you can see why I'm reluctant to invite her to dinner."

His brother blew out a breath of disgust as they stepped outside and into the overcast afternoon. The scent of imminent snow hung in the air, crisp and sharp. There would surely be snow before Thanksgiving.

"Did you apologize, or should I?" Reece persisted. "One of us needs to fix this situation."

"I apologized." Tucker turned and met his brother's gaze. Reece was one of the few people he could look in the eye without trying. "What else can I do?"

"I don't know, but you better think of something before Claire finds out. She likes Jena."

"You could fix it," Tucker said. "The ranch could be a designated sponsor of the holiday event that Jena is putting on to support the rescue."

"I can do that." Reece brightened and pushed his Stetson to the back of his head. "I just can't buy a building I'll never use."

"Great. But you have to talk to Jena like it was your idea. She won't let me have anything to do with the event, either."

"Shut you out of that, too?"

Reece was spot on, once again, though Tucker wasn't eager to admit that to his older brother. Jena had shut him out of the Jingle Paws events, and it hurt. Things between him and his partner were changing faster than he could keep up. It seemed everything he did was wrong these days and he didn't know how to get things back the way they used to be.

Tucker started walking toward his truck. "So, have you heard from Kate? Is she coming for Thanksgiving?"

Reece chuckled at his obvious change in subject. "No, but she'll be here for Christmas."

"We'll miss her at the Thanksgiving table. No one to fight with for the wishbone."

"Good news is that she wants your house."

"My house!" Tucker opened the door and placed his bag in the passenger seat before facing his brother.

"You won't be living in it." He shrugged. "She wants to know when she can move in."

"I haven't moved out yet," Tucker sputtered. Moving out of the house he and Megan built was part of the process of getting on with his life. He just hadn't had the reality hit him in the face until now. "Kate told you she's moving back and settling down? Like for good?" Tucker asked.

"Kate is thirty this year. Something about that number makes all rodeo professionals start thinking about how many more years they want to abuse their bodies and live on the road making peanuts and eating fast food."

"So you made all that up."

"No. I really think this is the year and when I told her your house would be empty, she seemed interested."

"Really?" While he was thrilled at the idea of Kate coming home, Tucker didn't miss the irony that she'd be walking into the family arms as he walked away.

"Trust me on this. Kate is coming home. We've been waiting for this to happen for years. It's happening." Reece paused. "I guess she can stay at my place until you leave. When is that, exactly?"

"You in a rush to get rid of me?" Tucker shot him his best indignant look.

"No. I've just resigned myself to the fact that you're going to do this whether I like it or not, and now I'm working hard to make the best of things. All in my favor, of course."

"Of course."

Reece crossed his arms. "By the way, I reached out to a friend of mine about the equine practice."

"You really are opening the barn door and shoving me out." Funny how when it was his idea, it was all good. With Reece onboard he'd gone from good to nervous.

"Merely thinking of my interests. You leave and I'm out a vet. I have a lot of animals on Rebel Ranch to consider. I need to know I'll have someone I can rely on to look after them. So I called Finn Hardy and told him about the opportunity."

"Finn Hardy. From Skiatook? How do you know him?"

"Old drinking buddy of mine, before we both found the Lord and a pew in Sunday church."

"How do you know he would be interested?" Tucker rubbed the back of his neck, not surprised to realize that his head was now throbbing.

"I ran into him at a trade show in Denver in October and we got to talking. He was getting out of a bad breakup and keeping his eye out for a change of scenery. I gave him a quick call this week." Reece narrowed his gaze. "You should be pleased."

Yeah, he should be pleased. Everything was working like clockwork, getting him closer and closer to Texas, except now that it was, he was starting to have doubts, which made no sense.

"Isn't that the Rebel Vet van coming up the drive?" Reece asked.

Tucker squinted to watch the logo van come up the road and into the circular drive in front of the Rebel Ranch main house, where the ranch offices were located. "It is." He nodded. "Oh, it's just Jena."

"Just Jena? I imagine she wouldn't appreciate the moniker."

"Oh, hey, you know what I mean. Jena. It's Jena."

"You sure don't know women." Reece chuckled. "Not a one of them wants to be labeled 'just' anything."

"Aw, it's not like that. You know Jena and I are buds. Most of the time I forget she's a woman."

Reece grimaced and shook his head. "You did not just say that."

Tucker clamped his lips shut, fearing his boots might jump into his mouth.

"Guess you haven't heard that there's quite a few fellas in town smitten with your 'just Jena.'"

"Really?"

"Yep." Reece grinned as though he was privy to an especially good secret.

Tucker ignored him while he tried to wrap his head around what was basically gossip. Sure, why not? Jena was a beautiful woman, even if he did forget that fact on occasion.

Jena hopped out of the vehicle, a smile lighting her face, which was always a good sign. "Hi, Reece. Happy Monday."

"Back at you, Dr. Jena. Good to see you."

"Thank you. You, as well. Tucker, the delivery guy dropped off several boxes of supplies for the equine clinic. I thought I'd deliver them myself."

"You didn't have to make a special trip."

When she full-on grinned, Tucker finally relaxed. He wasn't in the doghouse. Always a good thing.

"I've got the proofs for the posters and the flyers." Jena pulled a folder out of the truck. "I couldn't wait to show you."

Reece did a double take at the sight of Tucker and Ernie on the festive holiday poster. "Whoa! How did you get him to pose like that?"

"Dog treats were promised."

"Tucker eats dog treats?"

Jena burst out laughing, her dark eyes sparkling with humor.

"Very funny," Tucker said.

"Dr. Jena, I'm glad you stopped by," Reece said. "I want to apologize for my brother."

"Excuse me?" Tucker blinked and stared at Reece. Things were going fine. Now his brother was going to open a can of worms for no good reason?

"I'm speaking to Dr. Jena." Reece offered Tucker his back and turned to her. "I hope you weren't offended because Rebel Ranch is unable to purchase the building. I know you're in a bind."

"Not at all." Jena tensed. Her gaze skipped right over Tucker as annoyance replaced the humor in her eyes. "Tucker spoke out of turn," she continued. "It isn't his job to save the building."

"Exactly what I told him. However, I have to tell you, I'm excited about this holiday event coming up and Rebel Ranch would like to participate."

"Well," she said with a tentative smile, "we do have a few sponsorships available."

"What does sponsorship entail?"

"There are several levels." She pulled a form out of the folder in her hands.

"This." Reece pointed to the middle of the form. "We want this."

Jena raised her eyebrows in surprise. "You want to be a gold sponsor?"

"Our name and logo will be on the tote bags and the program, correct?"

"Yes, sir. One entire side of the tote bags will be dedicated to Rebel Ranch, and you'll have a full-page ad in the program booklet."

"I like the sound of that. I'll have a check sent over tomorrow."

A stunned-looking Jena smiled. "This is really lovely. Thank you, Reece."

"My pleasure."

Tucker nearly groaned when his brother flashed his trademark smile.

"Tucker mentioned a dinner dance?" Reece asked. "Where is that being held?"

"The community center," she said.

"Why not use our reception hall? We use it for weddings, corporate events and family reunions. It has an industrial kitchen and a stage. The place stays booked from spring through autumn."

Jena looked from Reece to Tucker. "Oh, I'm not sure we can afford that."

"Rebel Ranch is a sponsor, right? I'll donate the facility for the event. Tucker, why don't you take Dr. Jena out to see the place? See if it meets her requirements."

"Thank you, again, Reece," Jena said.

"Rebel Ranch is always happy to support local

businesses." He turned to Tucker. "You let me know what you two decide."

And Jena thought he was the family charmer? Not by a long shot. Tucker bit back a remark. At this point, he wasn't sure if he should deck his brother or hug him. Since Reece had managed to skillfully flip the situation around, he'd reserve judgment for the moment.

"Should we take the van?" Jena asked.

"We can use one of the ranch utility vehicles," Tucker said.

"This was really nice of your brother," Jena said.

"Yeah, he's…he's special, that Reece," Tucker muttered.

"Is there a direct road to this place?"

"Sure, but this is faster." He looked at her. "Haven't you ever been to the reception hall? You know, like for a wedding? We've had lots of weddings there."

"You know I'm not a people person."

"Right. Right."

Jena followed him to the other side of the barn where a bright green UTV was parked with its full-door enclosures in place for the winter.

They climbed in and Tucker started the vehicle, then turned up the heater. "You going to be warm enough? These little heaters aren't much."

"I'm fine." Jena glanced around the UTV and he did, as well.

How come he'd never noticed how small the interior of these things were before? He was inches from Jena, and he could smell a fragrance. Very nice. "Coconut?"

"Hmm?" She turned to him. "Coconut? Oh, must be my shampoo. I don't wear perfume."

Tucker nodded, unsure what to say to that bit of personal information. He wasn't even sure why he'd opened his mouth to start with.

They were silent for several moments as Jena took in their surroundings.

"What if it's snowing?" she asked. "Will the ranch road be open?"

"Oh, yeah, of course. We have our own plow. It'll be open."

Jena's gaze scanned the various structures dotting the landscape. "Rebel Ranch really has expanded."

"When was the last time you were out here?"

"I can't remember. Your brothers always assist when you need an extra hand."

He glanced at her as he backed up the vehicle. "You've never been to an event at the ranch either?"

"Which events would that be?"

"Reece opens the ranch twice a year. Once in the spring for a hoedown and then again for the fishing derby. Didn't you go to the big fundraiser that Mitch and Daisy did for the town the summer before they got married? The dinner dance was held out here."

"I remember that," she murmured. "But no."

"Huh." That was all he could come up with in response. He knew Jena was an introvert, but he hadn't understood exactly to what degree before now. It pained him to realize he'd been so oblivious.

As he steered the vehicle to the right, the beep-beep of construction vehicles backing up filled the air from the neighboring property.

"What's going on over at Ballard Farm?" she asked.

"Reece's wife still manages the orchards, and they're turning the homestead into a bed-and-breakfast. I think he said the drive is being paved today."

"A bed-and-breakfast?"

"Yeah, I'm sure I mentioned it to you."

"I don't recall." She cocked her head. "Isn't that a conflict of interest with the guest ranch?"

"My brother tells me that the farm will offer a different experience. It's supposed to be a little more upscale, less rustic, to bring in a different clientele. Claire's been working on the place since they got married in September. It's opening this summer, just in time for the tourist season."

Tucker drove the utility vehicle past Rebel Pond and across a pasture, then finally pulled into a parking area near a flat building. "On the left is the chapel. That flat building is the reception hall. Come on. Let's go inside."

"Is that a gazebo back there?"

"Yeah. They use it for photo sessions when it's warm. Those redbuds fill out nicely come spring and provide a really pretty backdrop."

He unlocked the door of the building and disarmed the security system. When they stepped inside, their boots echoed on the hardwood floor.

"Wow, look at this place," Jena said. "There's even a little stage. We could have the dinner dance here and put the band up on the stage." She did a graceful pirouette on the dance floor. He recognized the move from his sister's ballet days. Except Jena was a natural while Kate fared much better in the saddle.

Tucker stared, mesmerized, as she turned in a circle like a tiny ballerina. Even bundled in a winter coat, she managed elegant movements with practiced ease. "You can dance. I thought your talent was climbing trees."

"They aren't mutually exclusive. I can dance *and* climb trees." She stopped and shrugged.

"I didn't know that."

"Mmm-hmm. Ballet was my first love. Before animals."

"What happened?"

"Life." A shadow of sadness crossed her face before she turned away, dismissing the topic. "Do you know any local bands?"

Tucker frowned, wondering what she had omitted in her explanation, knowing now wasn't the time to press her.

"Bands in Rebel? Let me see," he finally said. "You mean besides the washboard bunch that performs at the Lonesome Dove on the weekends?" He shook his head. "Not offhand. How about a DJ? Someone who will appeal to all age groups?"

"I don't know." She looked around again. "I'm thinking that a guy in sunglasses spinning remixes of songs most of this town has never heard of isn't going to work for the event."

Tucker laughed. "You really don't get out much, do you?"

"Are you saying that you know a DJ?"

"The ranch has someone they recommend for their events. I can check."

"That would be great. Thank you." She glanced around at the bare tables and chairs. "Ugh, I'll need table linens and place settings."

"Ask Pastor Tuttle if the church can donate. He's a pushover for a good cause."

Jena nodded with enthusiasm. "Yes. Yes. I can't believe I didn't think of that."

"If you ask nicely, Mrs. Tuttle will rally the church ladies to serve dinner and do kitchen cleanup."

"You mean if *you* ask. I'm working on my social skills, but I haven't graduated to charming. That's your department, Dr. Blue-Eyes."

He cringed. "Do you have to call me that?"

"If the moniker fits…" Jena laughed.

Tucker stared for a moment, lifted by the sound. Why hadn't he ever noticed how her eyes sparkled and her smile lit up her face when she was having fun? And she was definitely enjoying teasing him.

"I think you're charming," Tucker said.

"Nice try." She walked around the room examining the pass-through window from the kitchen and the overhead lighting. "But no. That's definitely your lane."

"Okay, fine," he said. "I'll ask her."

"Thank you."

"What about table decorations? Flowers?" he suggested. "Or maybe jars with dog treats? I saw that in a magazine in the waiting room."

"I hadn't even considered…" Jena turned around and frowned. "My budget won't stretch to include table decorations."

"Maybe Rebel Veterinary Clinic could be a sponsor and cover that."

Her shoulders relaxed, and she offered a wobbly smile. "Oh, Tuck, I've been so cranky about doing it on my own and now you're offering to find a way for the clinic to help?"

"You were right. I threw you under the bus. I came back from Texas only thinking about myself and expecting you to just fall in line."

Yes, he was an extrovert, but that didn't excuse

the fact that he had spent most of their friendship running herd over Jena. He'd failed to respect her as an introvert and he now regretted that deeply.

She was silent as he spoke.

"We're a team, Jena. Look at how well we brainstormed this together."

"You're the one coming up with all the answers."

"You have the great ideas and I have a few solutions. That's teamwork. It works because we work. Our friendship works. Please, let me back on the team."

"Team Tucker and Jena."

"No. Team Jena and Tucker." He couldn't help but smile. "So, can I tell Reece that you'll use the place?"

"Yes. Please."

"There's one more thing, Jena."

"What?" She cocked her head and looked at him.

Did he dare take a chance now that he was back in her good graces and had been sufficiently and sincerely apologetic?

"Will you come to Thanksgiving dinner at Reece's house?" The question slipped out before he had a chance to weigh the wisdom further.

Jena blinked, as though taken off guard. "Oh, I don't know. It's your family. Not mine. I think I might have said that a few times over the years."

"Yeah, you have. But this is my last Thanksgiving in Rebel as a local."

"You'll be a Texan." Jena shuddered.

"Cut it out," Tucker said. "I'm actually serious here. Reece and Claire invited you because they think you're like family. So do I."

"Let me think about it." She walked to the door. "Come on, I have to get going. Ernie is overdue for a walk and I have animals to feed."

Jena reached for the light switch at the same time he did. For a moment, his large hand covered hers. Their eyes connected and Jena's brown eyes grew round. Her lips parted in a soft circle of surprise.

It seemed only natural to lean his face closer to hers. When he realized what he was doing, he stepped away, confused.

What just happened? His mind reeled. He'd almost kissed Jena and it seemed right. Absolutely right.

As they walked out to the UTV and got in, his thoughts kept returning to Reece's words. She wasn't 'just' Jena.

No, she wasn't, or his heart wouldn't still be banging in his chest.

Tucker was silent as he drove the vehicle over the bumpy ground of the pasture land. As hard as he tried not to overanalyze the incident, it was near impossible with Jena inches away.

"How many head of cattle do you have?" She

pointed to the small herd that grazed on hay in the distance.

"Oh, maybe a dozen. It's all for the ranch guests. You know, the complete Western ranch experience."

She nodded and turned to him as a rough wind shook the vehicle. "Even in November, with the trees barren and the ground brown and dry, there's an austere beauty to the land. Aren't you going to miss all this?"

"Now you sound like Reece."

"I'm not trying to. But you have something I'll never have here at Rebel Ranch. You have family and history, and you have the land."

"I know. Believe me, I do know how fortunate I am. I know how hard my brothers have worked to make this place successful. But all of this means more to them than it does to me. Rebel Ranch is just a place to me. I was away at college and then vet school when Reece first started. After that, you and I were launching the clinic."

He took a deep breath. "My home, my real home, was that trailer park where I grew up. I feel more attached to that old double-wide than I do this place."

Tucker paused. He'd never admitted this to anyone, yet now that the floodgates were open, he couldn't stop. "Don't get me wrong. I get Rebel Ranch is Rainbolt heritage. The land was my grandfather's. But I hardly knew him and the connection isn't the same for me. I don't have the same emotional bond to this land that Mitch and Reece do. All I ever wanted was to be a vet and now even that is a little empty."

"You lost your wife and your brother. That's understandable."

"No. The Lord guided me through that." Tucker shook his head. "It's this uncertainty that's getting to me. The only thing I'm sure of is that I can't spend another five years in limbo. I have to figure out what I'm going to do with the rest of my life. Stepping out and taking the offer in Texas is a start."

He tightened his grip on the steering wheel. "I feel like I'm so close to figuring things out and then I'm not."

"I hope you find what you're looking for," she said. The words were spoken softly and with emotion.

Tucker dared to turn his head and meet her gaze. "Me, too, Jena. Me, too."

Jena pulled open the back door and headed down the hall of the clinic. "Thank You, Lord, for Friday," she said under her breath. The week had been one of the busiest on record, especially since Tucker had been out of the office the last few days because the girls were sick. Appointments in the clinic were nonstop. It seemed that pet skin conditions, ear infections and eye issues were rampant in Rebel.

She'd almost been glad to have him out of the office. It kept her from thinking over and over again about that almost-kiss last week. Is that what it was or had she imagined it?

Well, she better get used to busy. This was what it would be like when he was gone, unless she could find someone to replace him.

She'd already made two house calls to Tucker's regular patients by the time she stepped into the break room on Friday morning. Now she was desperate for coffee, well aware that she'd have to make a pot herself. Many intelligent people worked at the clinic, however none of them understood the importance of brewing a pot when you take the last cup.

Jena stopped in the doorway. The carafe was full, and the familiar blue-striped box of Eagle donuts sat on the counter. "What?"

"Everything okay, Dr. Harper?"

She swung around. Dee stood at the refrigerator putting away the creamer. "Yes. I'm merely hallucinating." Jena waved a hand toward the coffee and donuts. "Where did these come from?"

"I picked them up on my way in. I hope you like glazed."

"Oh, I don't think I ever met a donut I didn't like and glazed are right up there at the top, battling for first place with Boston cream." She smiled. "You made the coffee, as well?"

"I did."

"You know, I'm accustomed to an empty pot. I'll need a moment of silence to process."

Dee laughed, a sweet laugh that gave Jena pause. Even her laugh seemed familiar. Why was that?

Jena reached for the carafe and poured a cup, immediately sipping. "Ah, bliss. Thank you." She looked at Dee. What a blessing it was that this particular young woman had come to the clinic looking for a job. Despite her blue hair and quirky fashion, Dee fit right in, as though she'd been there forever. She'd pitched in this week, assisting wherever needed, including helping Nolie with the phones. Today made it clear that she also understood the importance of coffee maker etiquette. Bonus points for the new hire.

"I'm so glad we found you," Jena said.

"I'm glad, too." Dee smiled and looked away, seeming almost uncomfortable.

"What are you doing for Thanksgiving, Dee? Going home?"

"No. My father is flying to California to spend Christmas with his side of the family. I'm not going."

"You're aware that we're closed after one p.m. on Wednesday and don't open again until Monday, except for emergencies, right? I mean, if you need more time off, we can arrange that. I have a few college students who are putting in part-time hours over the holidays who will fill in if you leave."

"No. I'm fine. I don't want to go to California. He and I don't see eye-to-eye right now, so it's best to have distance. I'm sure it will sort itself out eventually."

Jena understood the need for distance too well. "Is there something you want to talk about?" she asked gently.

"Not right now, thank you." Her voice was unsteady as she said the words.

Though Jena didn't want to pry. She did understand what it was like to feel as if there was no one to confide in.

"I'm here if you need to talk." She glanced at the college catalog on the break table and looked up at Dee. "Are you going back to college?"

"Not yet. I need to work." She nodded toward the catalog. "It came in the mail for the clinic and Nolie said I could look at it."

"Ah. Got it." Jena paused. "The clinic has a fund we established years ago for tuition assistance. It's not a lot but would certainly pay for a few online college classes during the spring semester. Or you could think about the vet tech certification program this summer."

"Really?"

"Sure. We usually work out an arrangement

where the applicant agrees to stay at the clinic working in return."

"I don't need to sign anything. I love working here."

"Yes, but once you get an education under your belt, you'll be a hot commodity. And who knows, you might want to go to vet school."

"I hadn't considered that, but wow, it would be great to work here with you and Dr. Rainbolt."

Jena smiled. "Why not? I like that idea." If only Dr. Rainbolt wasn't leaving.

Dee cocked her head. "Why would you do that? Help me like that?"

"We're family here at the clinic. Pilar received tuition assistance from the clinic when she first came to work for us. Family supports family. Right?"

"Family," Dee murmured with unsure eyes. "Um, Dr. Harper, there's something I probably should tell you."

"Pizza is here," Nolie called out as she strode down the hall toward them with boxes in her hands. "I smell anchovies. Come and get it. We have appointments in thirty minutes."

Jena looked at Dee. "Can it wait until after our staff meeting?"

"Sure. Sure."

"I'll be right back," Jena said. She slid past the receptionist and headed to her office.

"Where are you going?" Nolie called. "Lunch has arrived."

"I need some papers for the staff meeting. Did you tell Pilar and the boys?"

"Yes. It's great to have the extra help during Thanksgiving break, but those young men really pack away the food. I ordered two more pizzas."

"Worth every penny," Jena said. "Oh, and can you call over to the rescue and round up the volunteers?"

"Will do." Nolie grinned. "I love the holidays."

Yes, the holidays were special at the clinic and the rescue. At Thanksgiving and Christmas, Jena and Tucker did their best to show the staff how appreciated they were. But this year would be bittersweet. Today was the day that they announced that Tucker was leaving.

She'd steeled herself for the reaction. Nolie would come apart and declare that the sky is falling. Once she had the news, the grapevine would be close behind. Then the phone calls would begin. As if it wasn't difficult enough counting down the days until Tucker left.

Jena swallowed past a lump as she ducked into her office and grabbed a stack of envelopes and a clipboard.

"Hey, Jena."

She looked up to see Tucker standing in her doorway. He looked good, if not a bit harried. His golden brown hair was tousled and his shirt collar was standing on end. Definitely not the norm for him.

A smile tugged at Jena's lips, though she schooled herself to appear casual. The truth was, she'd missed him the last few days. "Hey, Tuck. How are the girls?"

"Better. I started them at preschool at the church in September, and ever since, they come down with all sorts of interesting diseases." He ran a hand through his hair. "I'm sorry I left you in the lurch. I couldn't leave the nanny with two sick children."

"No worries. And I think the whole spread of germs thing is pretty normal with kids. Wait until kindergarten next year."

"Yeah. Funny you mention that. I enrolled them in a nice school near the college. I sure hope this works. They're leaving all their friends here in Rebel. And their cousins. So many cousins." He sighed. "I don't want them to grow up with a fractured psyche because I moved them away from family at an early age."

"Right. I can see Hazel and Ginger on a talk show outing you as a horrible parent who ruined their lives at age four."

Tucker's eyes widened and his jaw went slack.

"I'm kidding, Tucker. Four-year-olds are adaptable."

"That wasn't funny, Jena."

"Sure it was. So, what did the doctor say it was this time?"

"Virus du jour. He told me to relax and let it run its course."

Jena chuckled. "Sounds like good advice to me, Dad."

"I guess so. Today they're demanding cookies, so I figured the worst was over." He shrugged. "Did you decide about Thanksgiving?"

She cleared her throat. "Would it be okay if I bring a plus-one?"

Tucker jerked back and his mouth dropped open. "A what?"

"Dee. She's going to be alone."

"Oh, Dee. Yeah, sure. I'll let Reece know. He'll be happy to hear that." His eyes met hers and he offered an almost relieved smile. "I'm glad, too."

Jena returned his smile, her heart thudding beneath his scrutiny.

"Ready?" he asked with a nod toward the break room.

She handed him the envelopes. "Your turn this year."

"Got it. Thanks." He paused. "Hey, I almost forgot to tell you. Reece found an interested vet to take over the equine clinic. He'll be out any day now to take a look around."

"Wow," she said softly. This was really happening.

"Pizza's getting cold," Nolie called out.

"We're coming," Tucker returned.

"Hang on a minute," Jena said.

Tucker looked at her, puzzled.

"Your collar." Jena stretched on tiptoes to fix his skewed neckline. Her fingers accidentally brushed against his neck, making her chest tighten and her breathing stutter. "All set."

Their eyes met and they looked at each other before quickly looking away.

"Thank you," he murmured.

"No problem," she murmured back.

There was a low hum of chatter in the air as she and Tucker entered the break room. A few office volunteers they hadn't seen regularly since last summer were present, along with two part-time students returning for the holiday break. Everyone was in good spirits, as they filled their plates with pizza.

"I don't see any pineapple pizza." Tucker frowned as he opened several boxes.

"Uh-oh." Nolie grimaced and stepped back from him.

"Not seriously?" Tucker returned.

"I put in an order for a large anchovy for Jena and Dee." She grimaced. "And I forgot. I'm so sorry, Dr. Rainbolt. It will never happen again."

"I'll live. So long as you keep that anchovy stuff away from me."

"We've got plenty of pepperoni, Doc," Pilar said.

"Thanks. I guess that will do."

Jena placed her plate on the counter and turned to the staff. "We're short on time, so I'll get the meeting started. First, a big thank you," Jena said. "The stats on the adoption event are in. Thirteen animals were adopted. That makes room for more, and hopefully we'll be able to adopt out a few more at our holiday fundraising event, to make room for the spring kitten deluge.

"Which leads us to Jingle Paws, which is Nolie Parker's idea. Jingle Paws is set to be our biggest fundraiser ever. It will take place the second weekend in December. The clinic will be closed." She held up a clipboard. "I'm passing this around. Please sign up for a volunteer time slot. You are all invited to the dinner dance free of charge. Your guests will be charged regular ticket prices, since this is a fundraiser."

"The next order of business is Thanksgiving," Tucker said. He pulled the envelopes from his pocket and grinned. "We have gift certificates to Piggly Wiggly for everyone to ensure you have a great Thanksgiving meal."

"Really?" Dee asked, glancing around at the staff as if checking to see if this was for real.

"Sure. Dr. Harper and I have done this every year for seven years," Tucker said. He passed out the envelopes, one-by-one and shook the hand of each person in attendance.

Jena observed silently as Tucker spoke to each employee and asked about their holiday plans.

He was such a good boss and a genuinely caring person. Tucker had been that way since day one, when it was just the two of them and Nolie.

Those early days were even more precious than today. This was their clinic. They'd built it together. Now Tucker was leaving.

She was going to miss him. That was a given.

Tucker looked to her and she nodded. It was time to share with the staff the reality of the new normal that was about to settle on Rebel Vet and Rescue.

The scene before her blurred as Tucker spoke.

Nolie gasped and clutched her pearls. "Oh, no, Dr. Rainbolt," she whispered. "How will we manage without you?"

With her words, jumbled emotions slammed Jena full force, unexpected, like an Oklahoma tornado. After four years of college, another four of veterinary school and seven years of building the practice, he was going to be gone from her life. Forever.

Another wave of emotions hit her and Jena edged to the doorway. "Excuse me," she murmured as she moved past Nolie.

"You okay, Dr. Harper?"

"Yes. I forgot something. Be right back."

Jena rushed down the hall to her office and closed the door. She leaned back against the cool wood and closed her eyes. Yes, she'd forgotten something. Forgotten that this was bigger than simply missing Tucker. There was going to be a gaping hole in her life, and in her heart, in a few short weeks.

How was she going to handle life without Tucker Rainbolt?

She thought it was all about the clinic, but lately...lately she sensed something more. Was her heart tangled in the mess of emotions she was feeling? If so, she was in serious trouble, because Tucker was leaving. And there wasn't anything she could do about it.

Chapter Six

"Ready?" Jena asked Dee. She pulled her keys out of her pocket and fastened her seat belt.

Dee nodded. "Where does Dr. Rainbolt live?"

"His house is on the Rebel Ranch property. Mitch and Reece run a guest ranch there. You know, like a dude ranch."

"Got it. Let me see if I have all of this straight. Mitch is married to Daisy and they have five adopted children and twins of their own."

"Correct."

Dee held up her hand and rattled off the names of each of Mitch and Daisy's children on her fingers.

"Now that is impressive. I'm not sure I could do that."

"Reece is married to Claire and they have a daughter."

Jena nodded and then looked both ways at the

stop sign at Rebel Avenue and First Street before proceeding out of town.

"Then there's Dr. Rainbolt and Hazel and Ginger, of course. Kate, his sister, is the youngest Rainbolt, and she is single."

"Correct again. How long did it take you to memorize that?"

"I put notes in my phone."

"That works. You'll look like you're checking messages and instead you're reviewing notes. I should try that. It might make these social gatherings less phobic for me."

A comfortable silence stretched between them as Dee stared out at the scenery they passed on the way out of town, and Jena did her best to mentally prepare for the day. Her first close encounter with Tucker since last Friday's total fail.

She had done her best to appear normal when she returned to the break room after his announcement, but she suspected everyone knew she was upset. Or maybe not, because they were upset. The entire office had been tense and silent, like a giant sob waiting to erupt.

Since then, Tucker had given her a wide berth and had been overly chipper and upbeat in the office. He hadn't once mentioned Texas.

By the time Jena had finished mulling over the situation over the weekend, she was forced to admit that the dynamics between her and Tucker had evolved since that fateful trip to Texas.

She didn't understand it, but at some point she'd crossed the line and had begun to see him as a man and not simply her best friend. It was a dangerous revelation, but there it was, and she couldn't undo the domino effect of unexpected feelings that accompanied the discovery.

Today she sorely regretted committing to Thanksgiving with the Rainbolts. But she wouldn't disappoint Dee.

"That was some news Dr. Rainbolt gave us on Friday," Dee said. "Everyone was talking about it afterward."

Jena shot Dee a quick glance. Had she been reading her mind?

"You know. About him leaving," Dee continued.

"I guess that's to be expected," Jena returned. "Seven years is a long time."

"It is. I've caught Mrs. Parker crying several times."

"What?" Poor Nolie. Beneath her labile emotions and tendency to dramatize beat a pure heart. Magnolia Parker really loved everyone at the clinic like her own children.

"She told me not to tell you. But I figured you would want to know."

"Thank you. I'll speak to her."

"Aren't you totally gutted, Dr. Harper?"

Jena gripped the steering wheel harder. Gutted. That was an excellent way to describe how she felt and couldn't say aloud to the staff.

"I've had more time to adjust to the information, Dee." That was as comforting a response as she could muster at the moment.

"Still, it's like peanut butter without jelly. Or hamburgers without fries. I can't even imagine the clinic without Dr. Rainbolt and you working together. No one can."

"Change isn't always fun, but it's part of life. Everyone will adjust." And if she said that three thousand times without stopping, she might, too. This putting on a brave front was for the birds.

"I don't know if they will. I've only been at the clinic a short time, and it's hit me pretty hard." Dee shot Jena a doubtful glance. "What are you going to do, Dr. Harper?"

"I'm going to put one foot in front of the other and continue to serve the community until the Lord tells me otherwise."

"Yeah, sure, I get that." Dee looked at her, assessing. "You're awesome, Dr. Harper. The way you're in tune with the Lord."

Jena groaned. "Do not give me too much credit. I'm stumbling along like everyone else. More than everyone else."

They hit a pothole in the road and Jena reached a hand to keep the box on the back seat from falling off.

"What's in the box?" Dee asked.

"Charlotte Barnett shared her pumpkin roll recipe with me."

"Yum! Now I'm trying to remember who Charlotte Barnett is." She snapped her fingers. "Four-year-old terrier named Gus?"

Jena laughed. "Yes. That's right. You're becoming a real pro. Most of us remember the animals first and then the owners. Job hazard." She glanced at the pink plastic storage container on Dee's lap. "Are those your famous brownies?"

"Are they famous?"

"Absolutely."

A smile lit up Dee's face. "They were my mother's recipe. Not exactly a Thanksgiving recipe, is it?"

"It makes people happy. That's the important part."

"What's your favorite Thanksgiving food, Dr. Harper?"

Jena signaled left and turned onto the Rebel Ranch entrance road. "Anything pumpkin."

"Mine, too." Dee was silent for a beat. "Thank you for bringing me."

"I'm glad to have you. This is a little intimidating for me, so it's extra nice to attend with a friend."

"The Rainbolts are intimidating?"

"Being social is. I get nervous. Not quite a panic attack, but close."

"But why? Everyone loves you."

"I suppose because the only small talk I'm comfortable with includes cats and dogs. And the occasional ferret."

Dee chuckled. "I get that. My family is very small. It's always been my dad and my mom and me. A small but happy family."

Jena nodded. "No aunts or uncles?"

"They mostly live on the east coast, and my dad's brother is in California. That's where he is this weekend. That will be good for him." She sighed. "My dad is wonderful, he's just having a hard time adjusting since my mother died."

"So he's close with his family? That's good." Jena had felt bad about Dee staying in Oklahoma and the problems keeping father and daughter apart.

"Yes. My father and his twin brother were adopted. I was adopted, too."

"Oh." The words were a surprise, causing a mental chain reaction and the resurgence of an eighteen-year-old ache deep in her heart. Jena could only hope, as she had a thousand times before, that the child she gave up was loved as much as Dee was by her adoptive parents.

"I've always known," Dee continued. "My parents lost a baby when they first got married, so they've always been super protective of me. I try to remember that when my dad is being difficult. He only wants the best for me. Like I said, he's been through a lot losing my mom, but…" she shrugged. "But I'm an adult now and he's got to let me have my own life."

Jena nodded and listened with a sympathetic ear, because clearly, Dee needed to talk. Holidays, while a joyful time for most, were also a time to reflect on the past and on family. Those emotions could be raw and painful.

Family. The only person who'd loved her unconditionally was her great-aunt, and she was gone, so Jena definitely understood how the mix of memories and expectations made Thanksgiving challenging for the young woman sitting beside her.

"I'm sorry, Dee. I know today isn't easy for you."

"It's okay. This too shall pass. Right, Dr. Harper?"

Jena offered a bittersweet smile as she guided the car past the Rebel Ranch's main house, where the ranch offices were located. "It will, Dee. It will."

"Where does Dr. Rainbolt live?"

"That's his place." Jena pointed to the modest brick-and-clapboard ranch home. "And up ahead is Reece's house."

"That's Reece and Claire's house?"

"That's it. Looks like a hunting lodge or something, doesn't it?" The house boasted two stories with three chimneys and lots of stone and rough-hewn wood. Jena parked in front and opened her car door, grabbing the pumpkin roll before she climbed out. "Here we go."

The front door opened at the first knock, and Tucker stood there grinning down at them. "Our esteemed guests have arrived."

Tucker angled his head to meet Jena's eyes. "Stop looking like you're going to the gallows, Dr. Harper." He turned to Dee. "Hi, there. Happy Thanksgiving and welcome to Rainbolt Manor. Lord Reece is busy attending to matters of the kingdom, but he'll be along soon."

Dee giggled at his greeting.

"May I have your coats, please, madams?" Tucker collected the garments and hung them in the hall closet. "Dr. Harper, you look very nice," Tucker said.

"It's a new thing I'm trying."

"A new thing?"

"Yes. Looking like a grown-up." She smiled. "You're leaving the clinic, so I decided this was a good time for veterinarian number two, as I am referred to, to work on my social skill set and being a grown-up."

He frowned. "Could you refrain from using the word Texas or any reference to my departure today? My brothers get riled up very easily lately."

"My lips are sealed," Jena returned. When his gaze landed on her mouth, she regretted the cliché. The last thing she needed was to think about Tucker and lips.

He took the box from Jena and the container from Dee. "Allow me to show you the road to the kitchen. Prepare yourself. We'll pass the living room, but the kitchen is another five miles down the hall."

"I smell turkey," Jena said. She inhaled the savory aromas. "Cornbread dressing, too."

"Keep moving in the direction of the amazing smells," Tucker said.

"You're in a good mood today," Jena observed.

Tucker shrugged. "Free food and all my favorite people in one place."

"Wow. Some house," Dee said from several steps ahead of them. She pointed to a wrought iron chandelier in the living room.

Wow was an understatement. The place was all hardwood floors and expansive windows to take advantage of the unobstructed view. The color palette left her envious. She imagined paint samples called sunset, cabernet, carrot and pesto. They created a Western slash southwest decor. It was like a magazine spread except more inviting.

"How is it that this house is so lovely, yet it looks completely functional? It's warm and friendly."

"Got me, and it's even tidier than your house," Tucker said.

"Yes, but Reece and Claire only have one rescue cat and the dog they inherited from her father. This place can hold a few more animals."

"Either that or more children."

"Do you know something?" Jena's head shot up to meet Tucker's gaze.

"I have my suspicions. We'll see if they spill the beans at dinner."

Her heart swelled. Another baby for the Rainbolts. This was definitely a happily ever after for a family with a heritage of heartache.

"Where is everyone?" Dee asked.

"They're all here somewhere," Tucker said. "This place is so large that I've gotten lost twice." He looked at Dee. "There's no way you're going to be able to remember who everyone is. I recommend you simply nod and smile."

"Too late," Jena said. "She already knows the name of every Rainbolt in Rainboltland, from the little ones to the big ones."

"Impressive," Tucker said.

Jena winked at Dee. "Told you."

Halfway down a long hall, Jena turned to Tucker. "I've peeked into every room. Not a television anywhere. Aren't we watching the game today?"

"Oh, yeah. Reece has a media room."

"Media room?" Jena's eyes widened. "Not really?"

Tucker nodded. "Yeah, really."

"This is like visiting a rock star," Dee said.

"Nice table," Jena said when they neared a massive table in the dining room. It was set for dinner with an autumn-themed tablecloth of rusts and greens. Amber bubble glass goblets offset burgundy linens and matching burgundy dishes. Tiny orange and white pumpkins lined a center runner that ran the length of the table.

"Be sure to tell Reece that. He's having buyer's remorse," a familiar voice said from behind them. Everyone turned as Daisy, Mitch's wife, approached.

"Too big?" Tucker asked.

"No. Too small. The kids still have to eat in the kitchen."

The redhead offered a welcoming smile. "Happy Thanksgiving, Jena."

"Happy Thanksgiving to you," Jena returned. "Have you met Dee from the clinic?"

"I have. She comes into the bakery a few times a week."

Dee blushed. "Guilty. Your cupcakes, Mrs. Rainbolt. They're amazing."

"Aw, thank you!" Daisy's cell phone rang, and she pulled it from the pocket of her slacks. "Excuse me, I have to get this. I'll catch up with everyone soon for dinner."

Jena looked around. "Where are Hazel and Ginger and their cousins?"

"This is how organized Daisy is," Tucker said.

"Her oldest kids are leading arts and crafts in the playroom."

"There's a playroom, too? Maybe I should be working at Rebel Ranch instead of in rural veterinary medicine," Jena said.

"Yeah, my brother has turned hard red clay into a lucrative operation, hasn't he?" He shook his head. "Reece isn't just a pretty face. He's always been a whiz at numbers and finance. Who knows? He might have ended up handling portfolios in some financial services firm if he hadn't hit the rodeo circuit first."

"Really?" Jena was surprised to learn about this facet of the gentle and polite cowboy.

"I always suspected my brother was different when he started advising me to skip lunch, save my quarters and invest in mutual funds. Which would have been fine, except I was eight years old."

Jena and Dee both laughed at the visual.

"What's so funny?" Claire Rainbolt asked. She wiped her hands on a dish towel and smiled at the visitors to her kitchen.

"Tucker is telling Reece stories," Jena said.

"Oh, stick around. There are plenty of those floating around here, and most of them are true." Claire greeted them each with a hug. "I'm so glad you came, Jena." Turning to Dee, Claire cocked her head. "Delighted to meet you. And I have to say, you look very familiar."

"Yep. I keep saying the same thing," Tucker returned.

"A blue cartoon character?" Dee asked. "I get that reference a lot."

Tucker laughed. "No. It's something else. I can't quite but my finger on it, but I will."

Jena too glanced at Dee. She'd been saying all along there was something familiar. Now the answer really nagged at her.

"It's the hair," Dee returned, looking away. "Next month it will be pink and I'll look like someone else," she demurred.

"Maybe," said Claire with a smile. "Or maybe I'll figure it out."

"In the meantime, tell me how I can help, Claire," Jena asked.

"Oh, no. I'm fine here." Claire looked at Tucker. "Why don't you show them the patio? Reece's favorite spot."

"I can do that," he said.

"You're sure you don't need help?" Jena asked again.

"I'm sure. Everything is under control here."

Dee glanced longingly at the shiny silver machine with buttons and levers that sat on a soapstone countertop. "Would you mind if I pass on the tour? I'm hoping Mrs. Rainbolt will tell me about that espresso machine."

"I'd love to," Reece's wife said. "But you have to call me Claire."

"I feel guilty for not helping you," Jena said. She looked to Claire, hoping for an out, because the last thing she needed was alone time with Tucker.

"There's nothing to do here. I'm all caught up. Reece has been helping and hovering all morning."

"Was hovering code for something else?" Jena whispered when she and Tucker left the room.

"See, I'm not imagining things," Tucker said. "Come on, this way. You won't believe this view."

"I've done more walking in the last hour than I have all week," Jena said as she followed him to double glass doors. "Isn't it cold out there?"

"They have patio heaters. Radiant heat." He pointed to the tall hammered bronze heaters that stood sentinel around the perimeter. "I'll turn them on when we go outside."

Tucker held the door as Jena stepped out onto the stone-walled patio that overlooked Rebel Ranch. The entire pasture spread out before them. Conifers filled the landscape at the far end of the ranch. To the right, the rooftop of Ballard Farm was visible.

"I've run out of adjectives for this house," Jena said. "I imagine this view is stunning at sunset."

"Yeah. I love it here. If I stayed, I'd be tempted to build a house with a view like this."

"Don't you like your little cottage?"

"I could fill a bigger house with children and animals."

Stunned, Jena turned to him. "You want more children?" She didn't know why that surprised her, but it did, and it also warmed her to know he even considered the possibility. It was completely ridiculous that his words made her smile.

"Sure," Tucker said. "Kids are great. If I don't remarry, I'll adopt. That's the plan."

"The plan? There's a plan?"

"For some things." He stared out at the sprawling pasture before them for a long minute. Then he turned to her. "What about you, Jena?"

"I like your idea," she mused. "I haven't given it much thought, but you're right, there are plenty of children in the world who need a home."

She'd been afraid to think about children before this moment. In fact, she'd avoided thinking about the topic. After all, she'd blown her chance, hadn't she? Yet, listening to Tucker gave her hope. Why not adopt a baby, the way someone had taken in her daughter? The idea filled her with a new peace.

A buzz sounded, and Tucker pulled his phone from his pocket. "That's the dinner text. We better hurry or Reece will start without us."

He stood and looked at her. "You okay?"

"Yes. Very much so." She smiled. "Lead the way or I'm sure I'll get lost."

In the dining room, Dee stared at the place card

with her name in calligraphy. It put her between Tucker and Jena.

"Something wrong?" Jena asked from behind her.

"Do you mind if I switch with you, Dr. Harper? Claire and I are discussing recipes."

"Not a problem." Jena sat down next to Tucker, her knee bumping his. "Oops. Sorry."

"Tight squeeze, isn't it?" he asked.

"It's the high chairs, I guess." Jena assessed the end of the table where Daisy's young twins sat in identical high chairs positioned between her and Mitch.

"Daisy can see the kid's table in the kitchen from her seat." Tucker said. "Just in case there's an emergency."

"Oh, so it's strategic seating."

"Exactly."

"Maybe I should sit with the kids in the kitchen to make sure they eat their dinner. I'm really happy to," Jena said.

His face registered confusion when he turned to her. "I forgot you're an only child with little experience with cousins. Let me clarify."

"Please do."

"Have you noticed Hazel and Ginger haven't been around?"

"Yes, I was wondering when I'd get my hugs and kisses."

"Today you and I are invisible. It's all about

their cousins." He smiled. "This is exactly how holidays should be. All the cousins in the kitchen making memories and messes, which, by the way, is more important than cleaning their plates."

Laughter sounded from the kitchen, serving to punctuate his statement.

Tucker grinned. "They're having a blast."

"I guess so. Thanks for explaining."

She carefully placed her napkin on her lap while everyone was seated. The table was already laden with the Thanksgiving feast. Nearly every square inch was filled with covered plates of hot food. Two baskets sat on either end of the table, overflowing with buttery rolls.

Jena glanced across the table and out the floor to ceiling window at the sky. "Look at those clouds that just rolled in. Snow tonight."

"Forecast is for clear skies and warming temperatures," Tucker said. He passed her the rolls.

Jena placed one on her plate and passed the basket to Dee. "Tonight. Snow," she said. "Count on it."

"If you're right, which you won't be, I'll come and shovel your walk." He handed her a bowl of mashed potatoes.

She laughed as she scooped up a serving of potatoes. "And if I'm wrong?"

"You can stop by my house and make dinner for me and the girls."

"Okay, but you are aware that you're a better

cook than I am, right?" Jena handed Dee the potatoes, followed by a bowl of stuffing.

"Doesn't matter. I'm sick of my own cooking."

The sound of a fork clinking against a water goblet had everyone turning to the head of the table. Mitch cleared his throat.

"Before we start this meal, let's give thanks."

"Okay," Reece said, "but no sermons. I like my food warm."

Jena held back a chuckle at the exchange.

"Bow your heads and take the hand of the person next to you, please," Mitch continued, ignoring his brother.

Around the table, all heads bowed. To her right, Dee took Jena's hand and to her left, she was keenly aware of her hand resting in Tucker's.

"Be present at our table, Lord. Today and always. We thank You for health and food, for love and friends. Bless these gifts and thank You that we may feast in fellowship with You. Amen."

A solemn utterance of 'amen,' spread across the room. When Jena looked up, she saw Reece wipe his eyes and smile tenderly at his wife. Mitch, too, smiled as his gaze took in each person at the table.

Jena turned to Tucker. "I don't think I've ever seen so much love in one room."

"Yeah," Tucker said, his voice oddly tight, "Rainbolts are amazing."

"I don't want to interrupt your meal," Reece said, "but Claire and I have an announcement."

Tucker elbowed her and she straightened with anticipation.

"We are about to welcome another member to our family."

"Dog or cat?" Tucker asked.

Laughter bubbled over and forks clattered.

"A baby, smart-mouth. Junior or Princess Rainbolt will be here about the same time as our mare drops her foal."

"Didn't waste any time there, did you?" Mitch said with a laugh.

"I'm not getting any younger. A couple years and I'll be an old man like you," Reece returned without missing a beat.

As the banter flew back and forth, Jena leaned close to Tucker. "How can you leave this, Tucker?"

He sighed, long and hard. "You have to stop asking me that, because I don't know the answer." His voice was rough with emotion.

Jena turned to him, and their gazes locked. "Thank you for inviting me."

Beneath the table, Tucker took her hand again. "I'm glad you came."

Her hand in his seemed right, even as her heart ached for something she couldn't define. She would take it one day at a time and not worry about tomorrow. Right now, all she needed to concern herself with was the loving people at this table and the man at her side.

Tucker sipped his coffee and glanced out the window. He couldn't believe it. Snow. He'd been up late last night, unable to sleep after their busy and emotional Thanksgiving. At no time had the sky given any clue that it was about to deceive him.

Ginger padded into the kitchen, her red hair standing on end. She yawned and pointed to the back door. "Pugsie wants out, Daddy."

She was right. Pugsley scratched and whined, his gaze moving from Tucker to the door. When he opened the door to let the dog out, a shower of snow flurries danced into the kitchen.

"Snow!" Ginger cried. Hazel was beside her in a moment. They snuck under his arm to stare at the winter wonderland their yard had become.

"I want snow," Ginger said.

Tucker barely grabbed the back of her pajamas only a second before she was able to get out the door. "We can go outside in a little while. When we do, you have to put on a coat and hat and mittens and boots."

He'd promised to shovel Jena's walk if it snowed. That was a flash of genius on his part. Mrs. Stewart was off for the holiday weekend, so Hazel and Ginger would be his shoveling assistants. This was going to be challenging.

"Is Pugsie cold?" Hazel asked.

"Pugsley has a fur coat. He'll come to the door when he's cold and we'll let him back in the house." True to his word, one minute later the chubby pug scratched at the door, his little corkscrew tail shivering. He wanted no part of the snow.

"Girls, we're going to visit Aunty Jena this morning."

"Yay. Aunty Jena," Hazel cried.

"I want breakfast," Ginger said.

"Can we see the Jingle doggie?" Hazel asked.

Tucker had prominently displayed the poster of himself and Ernie on the refrigerator and the girls were excited to meet her.

"Yes. Jingle doggie," Ginger added. "Pancakes first."

He could only laugh. Food motivated, Ginger always had her priorities straight.

Two hours later, he glanced with dismay at the pile of dishes and the pancake batter spread across the counter. Cooking with four-year-olds, while rewarding, was very messy. How did it take so long to get from pancake mix to wiping syrup off their mouths? And why did the kitchen look like an F2 tornado had blown through the place?

"Can't find boots," Ginger called from the hallway.

"Be right there, sweetie."

A moment later she was sobbing. "Can't find boots, Daddee."

Tucker grabbed her rubber boots from under the kitchen table where she'd left them and scooped the crying child up under his arm like a football. He headed to their bedroom.

"Hazel, where are you?"

"In the bafroom, Daddy."

"Do you need help?"

"No, Daddy. Hazel is a big girl."

An hour later, they were bundled into their snowsuits and in the cab of the truck in their car seats. The snow had begun to fall again, a gentle sprinkle of flakes as they drove past the main ranch house and out the gates of Rebel Ranch toward town.

He parked at the curb outside Jena's house so they'd have full access to shoveling her drive-way. Tucker eyed the drive. Thankfully, it was very short.

Once the girls were out of the truck, they began to run around the yard, catching snowflakes on their tongues.

Tucker kept his eye on them as he headed up the drive to the front door. When he rang the doorbell, Ernie's excited barks sounded, and at the front window a calico cat appeared.

A long minute later the door opened and Jena greeted him, soft and sleepy-eyed, her gray OSU sweatpants and sweatshirt as tousled as her short hair. "Good morning."

"You were sleeping?" He looked at his watch again. Nearly ten. He'd been up for what seemed like hours.

"Hey, don't judge. There was a marathon of Bing Crosby holiday movies on last night. I was helpless to resist." Then she glanced past Tucker and the twins to the sky. "It's snowing!"

"It's snowing," Tucker conceded.

"Yes! Snow for Christmas!"

"It's only the day after Thanksgiving," he said.

"At midnight last night it officially became the season."

Tucker wiped away an errant flake that landed on his face. "That prompted you to call the weatherman and put in an order for snow?"

Jena laughed. "No." She shivered, tugging her OSU sweatshirt down her arms. "It's cold. Come on in."

"We have a job to do."

Ernie barked and edged under Jena's arm to the door, where she sniffed the chilled air.

"Let Ernie out. We'll watch her."

"Okay, but you asked for it." Ernie bounded outside and raced in circles around Hazel and Ginger.

"Jingle doggie!" Hazel cried. She laughed over and over again, as she, too, ran in circles chasing Ernie.

"They're so happy."

"Sure, for five minutes. Seriously, Jena. We had four meltdowns just getting ready to come over here. These gals are creatures of habit, and they don't adapt well without Mrs. Stewart's schedule. What will happen when we go to Texas?"

"You cannot spend your emotional energy worrying about tomorrow. Today. Just focus on today." She smiled up at him. "Did you bring your shovel?"

"I did." Tucker smiled back. "Hey, and don't think I haven't noticed that the situation has flipped."

"What are you talking about?"

"Take therefore no thought for the morrow: for the morrow shall take thought for the things of itself." He raised his brows. "That used to be my verse."

"I memorized that when Charlie's letter came. Right before you went to Texas." She shook her head. "I had no idea how much I would lean on that verse in the month to follow."

"I'm glad." He did a head count and turned back to Jena. "Are you coming outside?"

"Did you miss the part where I said I just woke up?"

"You go have a cup of coffee and find your hat and mittens. I've got to keep an eye on these three."

A few minutes later she was outside.

"Did you have your coffee?" Tucker asked.

"It can wait. I want to play with my girls."

Like pastel marshmallows, Ginger and Hazel raced toward Jena in their puffy, quilted snowsuits. The ground was slick and their little booted feet kept sliding in the snow. When Ginger went down, landing on her bottom, she laughed and her hat fell off.

"Ginger, what is that in your hair?" Jena rubbed at the strands of white goop.

"Pancake," Hazel said. "She gots pancake in her hair."

"She has pancake in her hair?" Jena looked at Tucker. "What kind of trouble did they get into this morning?"

"All of it. Trust me. You should see the kitchen. I did my best to clean it up, but Mrs. Stewart is not going to be happy."

"What happened?" Jena raised her brows in question.

"We had pancakes for breakfast," Tucker said.

"I okay," Ginger said. "I okay."

Jena laughed and helped Ginger adjust her hat. She straightened and looked at Tucker. "She's okay."

Tucker chuckled.

Wanting to be part of the fun, Ernie licked Ginger's face and rubbed her snout against the child's hand, begging to be petted.

"Ernie likes you, Ginger."

"I like Ernie," Ginger said. "Daddy, I want a doggie."

"Let's build a snowman," Tucker said.

"I'll have to remember that distraction technique," Jena said with a laugh.

"It's the only way I stand a chance. Sometimes I just yell out random words to distract them. It works."

Jena began to laugh uncontrollably. "That's hilarious."

"I'm glad you find my life so amusing." He looked at the lawn where they'd shoveled most of the snow into piles about two-feet high. "There isn't that much snow."

"That's okay, we can make a small snowman. Maybe you can borrow some snow from my neighbor's walkway."

"Borrow some snow? Are you serious?"

"Yes. They won't mind. You do that part and I'll handle Frosty construction. But we better hurry. The girls aren't going to last very long. First snow of the year is wet."

An hour later they stood admiring Jena's snowman. Hazel was in Jena's arms and Ginger in his.

"C-cold, Daddy." Ginger shivered, her teeth chattering.

"Let's get hot chocolate," Jena said. "We can put their mittens and snowsuits in my dryer."

"I like how you think."

"It gets better." She winked. "I have Christmas cookies."

"Jena, it's the day after Thanksgiving. How do you have Christmas cookies?" He looked at her.

Did she sleep at all? Or was he not the only one up last night thinking about how really nice the day had been and how perfectly Jena's hand fit in his when they prayed? Then he hadn't been able to sleep, wondering why he was only now discovering how both of those things made him happy.

"I told you. I watched holiday movies and then it was only natural that I was inspired to pull out my cookie cutters."

"I don't think I've ever been inspired to bake," Tucker said. He herded the twins toward Jena's front door.

Getting them out of their boots and mittens and coats left a trail of clothing from Jena's foyer all the way to the kitchen.

"Well, your house used to be immaculate," he said thirty minutes later.

"Immaculate is overrated." Jena smiled at the scene before her.

"This is nice," Tucker said. And it was. Nice enough that it had him thinking about how he could ensure that days like today and yesterday happened again.

"Yes," Jena said with a nod.

"Hot chocolate and Christmas cookies," Tucker said. "That's all it took to put them to sleep."

Ginger sat at the table with her head on her chest, a cookie clutched in her hand, while Ernie eyed the cookie.

Jena slipped the frosted treat from her fingers. Across the table, Hazel made no pretense of trying to stay awake. Her forehead was on the table and she snored softly.

"I better wake them up so we can get out of your hair."

"What's the rush?"

"I guess there isn't one." He smiled, once again adjusting to the feeling of rightness in the scene before him. "This was fun. We should do this more often." There. He said it.

"Tucker, you're leaving in four weeks."

"Yeah, right. So why didn't we do this more often?"

Jena shrugged. "Busy syndrome. We're always busy with the clinics and the rescue."

Hazel mumbled something in her sleep and Tucker smiled.

"Let's move them to my guest room," Jena said.

"I can't hijack your day off."

"Why not? Besides, I was only going to watch a movie." She looked at him. "What were your plans?"

He shrugged. "Studying for the licensing exam."

"Do you have your books with you?"

"It's all online. I have my laptop in the truck."

"Great. Get it and I'll put my Bluetooth in and watch TV quietly. You can study."

"Are you sure?" Even as he said the words, willing to leave, he longed to stay. Jena's house was warm and alive, and he wanted to feel that way, too.

"I'm going to watch George Bailey and the citizens of Bedford Falls. You can study while Hazel and Ginger sleep. I have chicken chili in the slow cooker. You and the girls are officially invited to dinner before you go home."

Tucker hesitated for a fraction of a second. "Normally, I'd say no, but only because I don't like to—"

"Ask for help? Admit you aren't a superhero?" Jena suggested.

"All of the above. However, since you make it sound so…"

"Easy?"

"No. Painless." He smiled. "I accept. Thank you."

She laughed. "Make yourself at home, Tucker."

Jena sat on one end of the couch with her woolen-socked feet propped on the coffee table and Ernie's head in her lap as she snoozed. Tucker sat on the other end. A half dozen throw pillows and a dog separated them, yet it was the most intimate he'd been with a woman in a long time and it couldn't have felt more right.

Tucker couldn't help but sneak peeks at her as she watched the movie. Jena was pretty and smart and so much more. Why had it taken him so long to realize how much he cared for her? And what was he going to do about it?

When Jena pulled her feet off the table and stood to stretch, Tucker removed his earbuds. "What's up?"

Jena rubbed her eyes. "Nothing. The movie is over."

"No. How long has it been?"

"Two hours and fifteen minutes. I'm going to take Ernie for a walk."

"Let me do that for you."

She shook her head. "Not necessary. Besides, Ernie and I want to discuss the themes from the movie."

"Themes? What themes?"

"Faith. It's all about faith." She smiled. "George Bailey thinks he needs to leave to do what he's called to do. But in the end, he realizes that by staying he can contribute to what is more important—community."

Tucker narrowed his eyes. "You got all that from the movie?"

"It's a classic." She grabbed Ernie's leash and followed her out the door. "This won't take long, it's cold out there."

Tucker stood and twisted at the waist. He walked around Jena's living room, first examining her bookshelf. They had many of the same books from college. Her fiction collection ran to romance and comedy, while his was thrillers.

The door opened behind him and Ernie burst in the house as though she was being chased. Jena strolled in behind her.

"That was a world record," Tucker said.

"She refused to walk, did her business and headed straight for the house."

An exuberant Ernie raced around the couch and shook off the moisture. She leaned against Tucker, her tail in motion, until it knocked Jena's Bible from the coffee table.

Both Jena and Tucker rushed to pick up the papers that slid out of the Bible when it hit the floor before Ernie could devour them.

"Is that everything?" Tucker asked. "Wait, there's a picture under the couch." He retrieved the faded photo and stared at it, astonished. Then he looked at Jena to verify what he thought he was looking at. It was a very young Jena holding a baby, while sitting in a hospital bed.

"This is you," he murmured.

Jena carefully slipped the photo from his fingers and eased down to the couch. "Yes. It's me. A lifetime ago."

He looked at her, waiting for her to continue.

"It's long story, Tucker." Her shoulders sagged, as though the weight of that lifetime ago pressed down upon her.

"I've got time," he said.

"I'm not the person you think I am." She sighed. "Tucker, I've made a lot of mistakes."

"Oh, good. I'm not alone then. Here I thought you were perfect. This is a huge relief."

"Tucker," she warned.

"Okay, fine. I get that this is serious, but you need to know that I'm not going to judge you. Whatever you have to say, I can handle. Unless, maybe it's really none of my business."

"You're my friend, so I suppose it is your business." Her face was wan, her dark eyes wide.

Tucker's heart ached for whatever it was that caused her so much pain. He took her hand. "Go ahead."

"I… I had a baby when I was sixteen." She looked straight at him, waiting for his reaction.

Jena anticipated my rejection. Realizing that was like a physical kick in the gut. Tucker grimaced.

"My parents disowned me and my great-aunt took me in."

Tucker stared at her, stunned. Not by the words but at how the words, flat and void of emotion, seemed to be disconnected from the heartache that had to be associated with such pain. It was as though she was talking about someone else's life.

"I'm sorry, Jena. That had to be incredibly difficult."

"Was it?" She angled her head to meet his

gaze. "Or was it the easy way out for me? Did I deserve such compassion?"

"Don't do that to yourself. You were a kid. Surely you see that?"

"I don't know what I see. The only thing I can count on is that I have to start over every single time someone I care about finds out what I really am." Her shoulders sagged as if in defeat.

"Those people don't matter. The people who matter love you unconditionally."

"Unconditional love? I'm not worthy. Tucker, I messed up."

"That's nothing but a lie, Jena." He blinked as understanding dawned. "You're devaluing yourself. You've been doing that since I met you." Tucker stared at her long and hard, trying to get through that shield that she'd wrapped around herself. Now he understood why.

"I guess you think your sins are special," he finally said.

She opened her mouth and then closed it, as if surprised by his words. He was surprised, as well. But there it was. The ultimate lie that had been chasing Jena Harper down since she was sixteen.

"We all fall short, Jena. All of us. We accept His forgiveness and move on. Isn't God's grace sufficient? He forgave you. When are you going to forgive yourself?"

"It sounds very easy in theory."

"Not theory. Faith. That's what it's called. Like

the rest of us, you have to take one step in faith. One step and then another." He paused. "Do you get what I'm saying?"

Jena released a sigh. "I hear you, Tucker."

"Good. That's all I'm asking." He peered closer, startled to see moisture in her eyes. "Did I make you cry?"

"No. I'm just…thinking about her."

"Her?"

"Yes. A baby girl. The pain, sometimes it happens out of nowhere and slices me in two." She shrugged. "Regret and sorrow."

"Yeah, that's how grief is. It hits at weird times. I'm doing fine getting over Levi and Megan's passing and then wham, out of the blue."

"Yes. Yes. Exactly."

"People tell you that you'll get over it, but that's not how grief works. You don't get over losing someone you love. You simply learn how to breathe again, and you keep moving forward."

Jena nodded. "She'd be eighteen this year." A musing smile touched her lips as she held up the picture.

"So you've had no contact?"

"No. My aunt went to her grave with the information. I begged for an open adoption, and she agreed. But in the end my aunt decided that it was best for both me and the baby to walk away and live our own lives."

He wasn't so sure that he agreed with that particular decision, but he understood the intent behind it. Her great-aunt was a good woman to take Jena in when her parents turned her out and to support her unconditionally.

"So you never tried to find out...?" Tucker asked gently.

"I'm a coward. I didn't."

"You are definitely not. Jena, I'm proud of you. You had tough choices. Yours was a selfless love."

She pulled in a shaky breath. "Thanks for being my friend."

"That's a given."

When she offered a wobbly smile, Tucker longed to take her in his arms and hold her, but he couldn't, because that would be his undoing.

Chapter Seven

Jena attached the fresh pine-and-juniper Christmas wreath to the front door of the Rebel Rescue on Sunday afternoon. She couldn't help but hum a cheery holiday tune from her latest holiday movie binge. Though the snowfall from Friday had nearly melted, the streets of Rebel still sang Christmas. The lampposts were decked with holiday banners and oversize ornaments and the tree in front of the community center had been generously decorated.

Impatient with the delay, Ernie tugged at her leash while Jena straightened the clusters of small pinecones and the green-and-red plaid ribbon on the wreath. "Sit," she commanded.

Ernie rolled over, begging for a belly rub.

"Note to self. Sign up for obedience class," Jena muttered.

"Nice dog."

Startled, Jena turned to see a tall cowboy at the door to the clinic, reading the sign.

"This pup is wily," she said. "She knows exactly the right moment to turn on adorableness."

The cowboy laughed.

"May I help you?" Jena asked. She couldn't recall seeing this particular cowboy before. He was handsome enough that she would have remembered. "Do you have a veterinary emergency?"

"Who, me? No."

She offered her hand. "I'm Dr. Harper."

"That's your name on the door," he said. "Nice to meet you. I'm Finn Hardy. I'm in town to interview for the equine vet position tomorrow."

"Great. May I buy you lunch?"

"It's Sunday. Your day off. I don't want to impose on your holiday weekend."

"In all honesty, you aren't imposing. I was headed there anyhow. Sundays are meat loaf day at the diner and I'm all in for meat loaf, mashed potatoes and gravy. Besides, I'm hoping you'll love Rebel and decide to take that position. It sure would make my life easier. So if I can bribe you with meat loaf, it's really not an imposition, is it?"

Finn chuckled. "Well, when you put it that way."

"I live very close by. Let me run Ernie home and I'll meet you at the Arrowhead Diner. It's on Main Street. One block over."

"I'll see you there. Thanks, Dr. Harper."

"Jena."

Ten minutes later, Jena and Finn had barely settled in their seats at a back table at the Arrowhead Diner when Nolie Parker walked in. Jena turned when she heard the familiar voice greeting diner patrons. Nolie's eyes rounded when they connected with Jena's. She waved before making haste in an effort to reach their table. In seven years, Jena had never seen Nolie move that fast. No doubt she was going to need the mentholated cream tomorrow.

"Dr. Harper. So good to see you out and about."

"Out and about?"

The comment flew right over Nolie's lacquered blond head. The mother of six grown children had already turned her complete attention to Finn.

Finn, in return, provided Nolie with one of his very nice smiles. The man did have a way about him. She'd give him that. He wasn't Tucker, but he definitely was going to set hearts aflutter if he landed in Rebel for good. Yes, this cowboy was a heartbreak waiting to happen. It was a very good thing she had been vaccinated against heartbreakers.

"Why, hello there. I'm Magnolia Parker. I run the Rebel Vet and Rescue. You must be new in town."

Jena nearly choked as the words drawled from Nolie's mouth. She ran the place, did she?

Finn stood up, removed his hat and shook No-lie's hand like a proper cowboy gentleman.

Nolie fairly swooned.

More points for the cowboy.

"It's a pleasure to meet you, ma'am. I'm visiting your fine town, looking into the equine veterinary position."

"Oh! That's wonderful. Well, I'll leave you two alone. Enjoy your meal." Nolie grinned with delight and shot Jena a wink as she turned to leave.

"Is that…" Finn narrowed his eyes. "No. It can't be. Is that Dolly Parton?"

"What?" Jena whirled around in her chair so fast she nearly fell off the vinyl cushion. "That's, um, the pastor's wife."

Saylor Tuttle sashayed across the room with a grin on her face. "Dr. Harper, so good to see you…"

"Out and about?" Jena suggested.

"Why, yes." She smiled at Finn. "I don't believe we've met. I'm Mrs. Tuttle. My husband is the pastor of our local church." Today Mrs. Tuttle's voice was laced with a double dose of sugar.

Once again, Finn stood with his hat over his heart. "Dr. Finn Hardy, ma'am. It's an honor to meet you."

Mrs. Tuttle turned to Jena and leaned in. "I was holding out hope for you and Tucker, but Dr. Hardy here is a fine young man," she whispered.

"I, uh…" Jena couldn't find a response.

"Carry on, you two," the pastor's wife said. "I'll see you in church, Dr. Hardy."

"Yes, ma'am."

Jena hung her head and sighed.

"Something wrong?" Finn asked as he sat down and placed his hat back on his head.

"'Something wrong,' he asks." She lifted her head and released a sigh. "This is a small town. By sunset it will be confirmed news that you're the new vet, and we're getting married and our first child will be named Albert."

"Albert?" He shook his head slowly. "I had high hopes of naming him Finn Jr."

Startled by his response, Jena burst out laughing.

Finn folded his arms on the table, bringing him closer. Close enough that she could see the mischievous twinkle in his dark eyes. "I'm from Prue. Population is less than four hundred. I get small towns and I like them."

"Then I guarantee you will fall in love with Rebel. That sense of humor you have will give you some mileage along with those manners. Your mama did a good job with you, Finn Hardy."

Once again, he laughed. "I like you, too, Jena Harper. Are you staying or do you have one boot out the door, as well?"

She toyed with the little ceramic Christmas tree salt and pepper shakers on the table. "I'm here until the good Lord has other plans."

"Glad to hear that. Now that I've met the welcoming committee, tell me about Rebel, Oklahoma."

Their server placed water on the table and took their order, providing Jena with enough time to consider Finn's question.

She leaned back in her chair, finally relaxing. "The town was founded by William K. Rebel. Rebel has a Fourth of July parade every year that honors him. The parade route goes right by my house. I love this town. If you can't find it in Rebel, do you really need it? is my philosophy. We're a close-knit bunch. Whether you like it or not. I've been here seven years, since the clinic opened. I wouldn't want to be anywhere else in the world."

"That's quite an endorsement."

"It's the truth."

"It can't be easy seeing your partner leave." He eyed her as if assessing the situation.

"Tucker is my best friend and I'm grieved to see him leave, but I care enough about him to want the best. If Texas is the best, then I'll do everything I can to make that happen."

Yes, she had that speech down so well that her heart barely ached anymore when she was done.

"You're a good friend. I hope Tucker appreciates that."

"I...um." She picked up the menu, not sure what to say to that. Did Tucker appreciate that? Most days, last weekend excluded, she wasn't even sure Tucker was aware she was around. Therein was the rub.

"I'm going to get along fine in this town," Finn said, with a deep sigh of satisfaction. "Sometimes you follow where the Lord leads you, trusting that he's taking you to the right place. I believe I've found my next right place."

"You haven't even seen the clinic. How can you possibly be certain?"

Finn pushed his hat to the back of his head with a finger. "No, I haven't, but I've got a right feeling in my gut. Never, ever discount those feelings, Jena." He looked at her and smiled. "Know what I mean?"

"Yes. I do." Jena stared blankly at the menu.

Finn was right. Sometimes you simply had to go with your gut. Since yesterday, her gut had continually reminded her how wonderful Tucker was. Jena had replayed Friday over and over in her mind. She'd opened her heart, and he hadn't walked away. He'd barely blinked when she'd told him about her past.

And now? Well, now her gut was telling her that she was falling in love with Tucker Rainbolt. She just had to figure out what she was going to do about it.

"Morning, Dr. Rainbolt." Nolie placed a huge poinsettia on the reception counter and put her hands on her hips. "Don't say it."

He turned from the schedule on the wall and met the blinking holiday earrings dangling from Nolie's ears. Christmas was game-on for the clinic receptionist. "Say what?" he asked.

"Every year I bring in a poinsettia and every year you remind me not to let the animals ingest the plant."

"I was just going to say good morning."

"Oh, well, then, go right ahead."

"Good morning, Nolie. How are you?"

"I'd be better if you weren't going to Texas."

"I appreciate the sentiment, and your loyalty the past seven years. This clinic is in business because of you."

Nolie stuttered for a moment, her face pink. "Why, thank you, Dr. Rainbolt."

"You're welcome. It's the truth. I'm replaceable, but you are not."

"Oh, now you're exaggerating." She grinned. "But you can keep going if you like."

Tucker laughed. "I would but I've got to get out to the ranch soon."

"With all your flattery, I nearly forgot to give you the latest news. I met Dr. Hardy yesterday at the diner. He was having lunch with Dr. Harper." She chuckled. "Dr. H and Dr. H. That's cute, isn't it?"

Jena and Finn having lunch? Tucker frowned. He didn't think Jena dated. Did she date? How

"Sure. Do you get a real tree?"

"No, we've tried that a few times. The dogs consider it their own personal fire hydrant, or they try to drink the water. It's just not worth the energy. We put up a tinsel one now and they don't go near the thing."

Tucker stared at Dee for a few minutes. Again there was that feeling of familiarity. It was fast becoming an urgency to figure out the puzzle.

Dee caught him staring and smiled. "Fresh coffee in the break room," she said. "I just made it."

"Great idea. Thanks." He put the mail down and headed for the coffee pot.

A few minutes later, Dee came in the break room and opened the storage room door. She stared at the top shelf.

"Need help?" Tucker asked.

"I'm too short to reach. I'll get the stepladder from Mrs. Parker."

"You and Dr. Harper." He laughed. "She can't reach that shelf, either. I'll grab them for you." Tucker easily managed to collect all the boxes from the top shelf. He stacked them neatly on the floor.

"Thank you so much."

"No problem. I appreciate how you pitch right in with everything at the clinic."

"I love it here." The sincerity in her voice was reflected in her eyes. She meant it.

"So Dee, how did you end up in Rebel?" Tucker asked.

"I stopped in at the Arrowhead Diner for lunch and saw the ad in *The Weekly Rebel*."

"Just happened to be in Rebel?"

"I guess I was feeling sorry for myself. I pulled out of my classes because I couldn't afford tuition after my mother passed. So I got in my car and drove from Tulsa."

Something didn't add up and Tucker was hesitant to push the questions further. He might end up with answers he didn't know how to handle.

She gazed at him, wary for a moment, then waved a hand toward the hall. "I'll just, um, I'll grab the hand truck by the back door and load the boxes up."

In that second, he knew. There was no doubt in his mind.

Dee is Jena's child.

For a long moment he was completely speechless, as his mind raced with questions at the revelation. His gaze followed Dee as she left the room and he realized that she even walked like Jena.

How had he missed it? The gestures and mannerisms that haunted him for weeks finally made sense. Now that he had his answer, what was he going to do with the information so no one got hurt?

Did he even have the right to make a call in

this situation? He'd preached to Jena about acceptance. He had no idea why Dee was here, and he wasn't about to rush to judgment.

Nolie stuck her head in the break room. "Dr. Rainbolt, that's your office phone ringing."

"What?" He shook his head, clearing his mind.

"Your personal phone is ringing."

"I've got it." Tucker jogged into his office and grabbed the receiver. "Dr. Rainbolt."

"Dr. Rainbolt, this is Theodore Leonard from the OSU College of Veterinary Medicine out in Stillwater. I haven't received your CV yet."

"My CV?"

"Yes, your brother said you'd have it over to us before the holiday."

"Which brother would that be?"

"Mitch. We both agreed you'd be the perfect candidate for an open position we're going to have at the college in the spring."

"You're calling from OSU?" Tucker sat down, attempting to ground himself.

"Yes. Maybe you'd like to schedule an interview and bring your CV with you at that time."

"That's a very good idea." Tucker grabbed at the idea until he could figure out what was going on here.

"It's really only a formality. I understand that we might be stealing you away from another university and we're more than willing to make it worth your consideration. It's a part-time instructional position at the moment, but I foresee an expansion of hours in the future."

"Sir, I am honored to hear from you, and honored by your offer to interview, but would it be possible to call you back? I've got an appointment." An appointment to throttle his brother, Mitch.

"Absolutely. I look forward to hearing from you, Doctor."

Tucker pulled out his cell phone and pushed his brother Mitch's number.

"Hi, Tucker. This is Daisy. What can I do for you?"

"Oh, sorry, Daisy. I thought I called Mitch's number."

"You did. He accidentally took my phone this morning."

"Is he around?"

"Mitch is in Tulsa today. He's searching for bicycles to put under the Christmas tree for the kids."

"Can you have him call me as soon as he can?"

"Oh, my. Is this an emergency, Tucker?"

"No, Daisy. Not an emergency. I'm going to give him a dressing down for meddling in my life. Plenty of time for that after he gets back from T-town."

"Uh-oh, what did he do?"

"You probably should ask him."

"Oh, Tucker. I'm so sorry. I won't let him have any pie until he calls you. Promise."

"Thanks, Daisy."

Jena appeared in the doorway. "Whoa, what's that look on your face?"

"My brothers have their boots all over my life again."

"It's pretty comical how they do that. You have to admit."

"You're an only child." He leaned back in his chair and clasped his fingers behind his head. "I used to dream about being an only child."

She laughed. "Hey, by the way, I ran into Dr. Hardy yesterday. I bought him lunch. It was the meat loaf special. He's all but packed his bags and moved to Rebel."

"Is that right?" He imagined Jena and Finn Hardy cozy in the diner and frowned.

"It is. So stop frowning. I was better than a used car salesman. You may thank me later."

Tucker couldn't help but laugh and just like that, his annoyance at Mitch and Finn disappeared. Jena was always sunshine in his day. "So are you swooning like Nolie?" he asked.

Jena scoffed. "He's cute, but not as cute as you."

Tucker flew forward in the chair at the remark. "It's a little early in the day to be messing with me."

She winked. "Am I messing with you?"

He narrowed his eyes, trying to figure her out and finally gave up. "I'm glad you're in such a good mood."

"Thanks to you, Tucker. I'm feeling much better about life in general. I wanted to thank you again for…" She shrugged a shoulder. "You know. Helping me to unpack a lifetime's worth of baggage. I feel like I should send you a check for therapy."

"Cut it out. You'd do the same for me."

"Yes, I would." When her mouth curved into a sweet smile, he found himself wondering what it would be like to kiss Jena's soft lips. He shook his head.

What am I thinking?

Tucker drove out to Rebel Ranch, his thoughts jumbled with everything that had happened that morning. He barely noticed the Christmas greenery that decorated the metalwork on the archway and gate to Rebel Ranch. Even the ranch house and the white fence in front of it wore garlands of fresh fir entwined with red satin bows.

A moment later, a black two-door extended cab with a bed the size of Texas pulled up.

"Nice truck," Tucker said when the cowboy stepped down and planted his boots on the ground.

"Thanks." He grinned. "You must be Tucker."

"Yeah, how'd you know?"

"Reece described you."

Tucker raised a palm. "I don't even want to know."

The other man laughed. "I'm Finn Hardy. Nice to meet you." He offered his hand and another grin, then glanced around. "This place is beautiful, and all dressed up for Christmas."

"Yeah, Reece manages the guest ranch with my brother Mitch. They've really made it a tourist destination."

"So I've heard." He nodded. "I'm really excited about seeing the clinic."

"I'm glad to hear that. Let's head this way."

"Tell me about your practice," Finn said.

"It's just me out here, though my brothers will lend a hand if needed. You can also count on Dr. Harper. She and I handle the small-animal clinic."

"I met Jena yesterday. She's a very interesting woman."

So it was Jena already? Tucker bit back annoyance. "Dr. Harper is the best," he finally said.

Finn chuckled. "I was going to say that, but I didn't want to seem too enthusiastic. She's a really great gal." He looked at Tucker hesitantly. "Is she dating anyone?"

"Excuse me?" Tucker was poleaxed by the question and, though he did his best not to show it, he felt sure Finn saw the surprise that shot across his face at the question.

"Sorry if I spoke out of turn. Nothing worse than a man trying to court another cowboy's sweetheart. I figured you might know since you two are best friends and all."

"I probably should stay out of Dr. Harper's business," Tucker answered. After all, wasn't he just this morning railing on his brother for stepping his boots where they didn't belong?

"Sure, okay, no offense intended."

"None taken." Tucker unclenched his hands.

"Who covers this clinic when you're away?" Finn asked.

"I partner with a large-animal clinic in Hominy for on-call duty. They're my choice referral facility for elective surgery, as well. They serve the livestock in the area. Except for Rebel Ranch, that is. I handle everything the ranch needs. It's a built-in customer base and in return, the rent on the clinic building here is rock bottom."

"I like this setup. I like it a lot," Finn said after they had toured the clinic and the ranch in the UTV.

"Glad to hear that."

Except for the remark about dating Jena, Tucker could find no fault in the vet. He had the credentials, he was good with animals and if Nolie and Jena's response was a reliable gauge, the cowboy was good with people, too.

"I'm going to kick around Rebel for a few days and visit my folks in Prue," Finn said. "Mind if I reach out with questions?"

"Not at all. Dr. Harper and I have an event coming up next weekend. Hang on, I'll get you a brochure." He grabbed one from his car and handed it over.

Finn chuckled and tapped the picture of Tucker and Ernie on the cover. "Nice picture."

"Yeah, they got Ernie's good side." Tucker grinned. "We'd love to have you join us. I can guarantee the dinner on Friday night will be memorable. The ranch chef is handling the menu."

"I'll do that. I appreciate the warm welcome." Finn took another slow look around, his gaze spanning the land. "You sure you want to leave this place? Seems like you have something special here." He shrugged. "I guess sometimes we don't know what we have until we don't."

Finn Hardy's words stuck in Tucker's mind long after his truck drove away. Why was it everyone seemed to have an opinion about his future? He barely knew the guy, yet he, too, offered unsolicited advice. Tucker rubbed his face with a gloved hand. Maybe he had a sign on his back that said *give me your thoughts*.

Tucker stopped by the stables and took a quick peek at Reece's mare. "Looking good, young lady."

"I hope you aren't talking to me." Reece popped his head out from a stall with a wheelbarrow in his hands. "Tucker, what are you doing out here? This isn't your regularly scheduled clinic day, is it?"

"I might ask you the same thing. Why are you shoveling stalls?"

"I gave a few of my hands extra time off for the holiday weekend." He leaned against a stall and wiped his face with a bandanna. "So what's going on?"

"Nothing. I just showed Finn Hardy around the place."

"You should have let me know. I would have given him the royal treatment."

"No need. Jena already did that."

"Jena?"

The wind blew through the half-open door and redirected the scent from the wheelbarrow straight to Tucker. He grimaced and took a fast step back. "That's strong stuff." Pulling his hat from his head, Tucker fanned the air. "I see you're busy, so I won't keep you."

"Where are you going?"

"I think today might be a good day for a ride. Mind if I take Dinkum?"

"Be my guest." Reece narrowed his gaze. "You still know how to ride?"

"You're a real hoot, Reece."

"I try."

Tucker grumbled under his breath. The Rainbolts were born in a trailer, but they all took turns hiring on at several of the ranches in town. Reece and Kate had followed after their daddy's footsteps and hit the rodeo. Thankfully, that particular passion had never run through his blood.

But yeah, he still remembered how to ride.

He ran a hand down the chestnut mare's neck and withers, spending a few minutes saying hello before he saddled the horse. Once the saddle was cinched and secure, he led the animal down the stable alley and out the door. The horse gave a gentle nicker as if to say, *Let's go, cowboy.*

Boot in the stirrup, he lifted himself into the saddle. With a cluck of his tongue and a gentle nudge, he and Dinkum headed to the worn trail along the pasture fence line. Tucker pulled up his collar and yanked his hat lower to keep the breeze from sliding down his back. He began to relax as he and the mare found a rhythm. There was something about a long ride that eased the tension in his shoulders and made his troubles seem insignificant against the beauty of Rebel Ranch.

Tucker took a deep breath. Change was coming. Yeah, things were getting real. Almost too real. Finn Hardy was a good fit for the equine clinic. That's what Tucker wanted, wasn't it?

The trouble was, when he came back from Texas, he'd been certain. Absolutely certain. Now the line between certainty and certain doubt was blurry. He didn't know anything anymore and could only pray that a long, cold ride in the saddle would tire him out enough that he could sleep tonight without thoughts of Jena chasing down his dreams.

Chapter Eight

Jena pushed open the door to the reception hall and placed the last box of ornaments for the Jingle Paws tree on the floor. She wiped her face with the sleeve of her sweatshirt and shoved her bangs back. It might be thirty-two degrees outside, but she was rapidly overheating from all the running around she'd been doing.

When the door behind her closed with a thud, Tucker turned. He gave her a nod of greeting and started across the room toward her.

She stared at him. Did the man not sweat? How was it that she was a mess and he looked like a commercial for some 'ruggedly handsome' aftershave with that tool belt around his waist and the shadow of a beard on his face?

"What did you bring this time?" he asked.

"Kitten and puppy ornaments for the tree," she replied. "Each one has a small paper attached, with an item on our shopping list for the rescue.

Our guests may take one or several home with them, depending on how generous they feel tonight."

"That's a great idea."

"I thought so when I borrowed the idea from a magazine."

He nodded to the front of her sweatshirt and jeans. "And what's all over you?"

Jena followed his gaze and then laughed. "Sparkles from those oversize ornaments we hung from the ceiling. I tipped the box over and it went everywhere." She dusted off her clothes with her hands.

"Well, now you've done it." Tucker leaned close, his sight fixed on her mouth.

Jena froze and held her breath. When she swayed away from him, he put a hand on her arm.

"Stop moving, would you?" He touched the pad of his finger to the side of her mouth. "Green sparkles."

"Thank you," she murmured. "All gone?"

Tucker nodded.

She reached for her clipboard and prayed the palpitations he'd set off when he touched her would stop soon.

"Did you do those centerpieces?" Tucker asked.

Jena nodded and admired the tables. The quirky centerpieces were made from fir wreaths that surrounded red-and-green beribboned apothecary jars filled with dog or cat treats.

"We'll give them away at the end of the evening."

"Jena, those are really clever," Tucker said.

"Thank you. It turns out I really like this party planning. Maybe if the vet gig doesn't work out, I'll become an event planner."

He shot her a look.

"What?" She raised her shoulders.

"Everything is going to work out," he said.

"I'm all for taking it day by day, but right now we need a reality check, Tucker. This is the second week in December. We have fifteen days left for everything to somehow fall into place." She shook her head. "I haven't given up hope, though. I have an appointment with yet another bank and I've got a lead on a commercial space in Rebel that will be available for lease at the first of the year."

"I'm looking at a few promising leads myself."

"I need more than promising, Tucker. Every day I wake up and say a prayer to remind the Lord that I'm not very good at living on the edge."

Tucker walked over to his backpack and pulled out a plastic container. "Maybe this will help."

"What is it?"

"Peppermint Bark."

Jena smiled. "My favorite. Pass that here, please and thank you." She popped a piece in her mouth and plopped down on the floor. "This is exactly what I needed. Sugar and chocolate."

"Where are all your helpers?" Tucker asked.

"Nolie has an appointment at Rebel Curl to get her naturally blonde hair enhanced and Dee is over at the community center. I put her in charge of the big bazaar and animal fashion show tomorrow. There was a dress rehearsal today."

"An animal fashion show dress rehearsal?" He laughed. "I saw that in the brochure and thought it was a joke."

"Not a joke. It's a ticketed event. All proceeds benefit Rebel Rescue. And all of our models are available for adoption."

"Jena, this is beyond great. I should have been pitching in more." He shook his head. "My only excuse is the exam. Which by the way, I passed."

"I never doubted it for a minute." She raised a palm for an air high five and eyed him. "You aced it, right?"

"Yeah," he murmured, looking suitably embarrassed.

"Are you taking the girls to the Jingle Paws bazaar?" she asked.

"It's like a Christmas market, right?"

"With free swag and a heavy emphasis on all things pet. Daisy's baking dog biscuits."

"How will that profit the rescue?"

"Table space fees. It's an easy off-the-top income and it's tax deductible for vendors who participate."

"Yeah, we'll pop in."

Jena glanced at her phone. "Break over." She stood and stretched.

"Before you start running around again, where do these lights go?" Tucker held up the string of lights from a large cardboard box.

"Ahh! The lights. I forgot the lights." She jumped up to the stage and wrestled the ladder down the steps.

"Whoa, I take direction well." Tucker appeared at her side and swiftly removed the ladder from her hands. He held it aloft with one brawny arm. "Point me in the right direction and I'll get them up."

"They go on the tree. I don't know what I was thinking."

"I can put up the lights and the ornaments." He looked her up and down. "Maybe you should consider heading home to get dressed."

Jena looked down at her jeans and sweatshirt. "Is that a commentary on my attire?"

"No, it's a plea from the man who needs your management skills when those doors open at seven p.m. and all of Rebel pours into this room." He leaned the ladder against the wall. "You're the management genius behind this event. I don't know what I'm supposed to do beyond smile."

"Oh, so this is about you." She smiled.

"Exactly."

"I can't go home yet." Jena tapped her clipboard. "There's the tree and I've got half a dozen things left on this list. And I haven't even passed out the candy canes. It's not a holiday party without candy canes."

She glanced around the room. "Another hour or two, tops, and I'll be done. I can't wait to see what this place looks like tonight with all the lights up and the music and people. Of course, I'll be hiding in the corner breathing into a paper bag."

"How many tickets were sold?"

"Let me look that up. Nolie's been tracking those numbers." Jena flipped through several pages on her clipboard. "We sold out." She looked up at him. "There's even a wait list."

Jena blinked, realizing that she was going to be leading a very large peopling event. She'd been joking about hyperventilating, but now? Now reality hit.

"Are you okay?" Tucker peered closer. "You look a little sick."

"I feel a little sick. This room is going to be packed. All those people in one room."

"You work the adoption events, and they're the same thing. A room full of people."

"And animals. That's the key. All those animals provide a buffer between me and humans. Plus, you're always there."

"I'll be there tonight."

"It's not the same. This is going to be wall-to-wall people. I might never find you in a crowd that big."

"I still don't get it." Tucker frowned. "You handled the co-op meeting like a pro. I don't get what the difference is."

"Clearly, you do not understand the rules of introvertism."

"Is that a word? Really?"

"Yes. Let's review. There were twenty, twenty-five people at that meeting. We're talking somewhere around eighty tonight. The co-op meeting was me sharing my passion for animals. This is—" she released a strangled sound "—much different."

"Your entire support team is here tonight. Nolie, Dee and Pilar will be there, too."

"If I can find all of you."

He put his hands on her shoulders, and they warmed her skin through her sweatshirt, more comforting than she would have imagined. "I'm always a text away."

The irony of his comment did not escape her. Three weeks until he left Rebel. Three weeks until there would be no more Tucker in his office. No traces of his aftershave when she walked down the hall. No more pineapple pizza on Friday.

She swallowed, pushing back her emotions.

"Hey, cheer up," he said. "You've done a great thing uniting the town for this event. I heard the entire Rebel Police Department is coming with their significant others."

"Yes. Sheriff Henna Eagle is coming with her husband, Will. Luna is bringing retired Officer Roscoe McFarland. Oh, and remember Officer Gallegos? He's bringing Pilar."

"This is all good news. Everyone is excited about the event and eager to support the rescue. Our Rebel friends support us."

"Yes, but you have to admit that it's a lot of pressure."

"Sure it is, but you're prepared, Jena. You've done nothing but eat, sleep and breathe this event for the last six weeks. I've never seen anyone as organized. What can go wrong?"

As he said the words, the room was plunged into darkness.

Jena gasped and then stumbled into him.

Tucker grabbed her around the waist. "You okay?"

Her eyes adjusted to the dark, and she felt his breath touch her face. "Yes. Thank you. You can let me go now." She shivered when he released her, already missing the warmth. What would it be like to have the right to have Tucker's arms around her whenever she chose? She sighed.

"What was that big sigh about?"

"That was my frustration at this glitch. I so hoped everything tonight would go smoothly. What do you think happened?"

"I'm going to guess it's something to do with

the work over at Ballard Farm. Jena, go home. I'll handle this."

"I can't go home until this is resolved." She was the boss now, and bosses did not go home in the middle of a crisis. The days of dumping everything on Tucker were long gone.

"The ranch has generators we can bring over if the problem isn't an easy fix, and Reece has staff to handle that." He pulled out his phone. "I'm texting him right now."

"Still, this is my project. When the lights come on, and my list is completed, then and only then will I head home."

Tucker snapped his fingers. "We could open the boxes of candy canes and put them on the tables while we wait," Tucker said. "Our phones have flashlights."

Jena pulled her phone from her pocket. "Right this way," she said.

Thirty minutes later, the lights blinked twice and came on for good. Then the front door opened.

"Anybody home?" Mitch called.

Mitch, Daisy, Reece and Claire came through the door.

"You fixed the electricity?" Jena asked the obvious.

Reece nodded. "Yeah, but we've lost valuable time for you. So we're all here to help you finish things up for the dinner tonight."

Jena held the boxes of candy canes tight as she stared at the group before her, humbled by their generous offer. She knew from talking to Tucker that each of them had triumphed over a rough past. They weren't victims, but survivors who overcame because of their faith.

She could learn a lot from the Rainbolts.

"You didn't have to do that," Jena finally said.

"Yeah, we did," Mitch said. "This is Rebel Ranch and we've got a responsibility." He grinned. "Besides, it's nearly Christmas. This counts as our holiday goodwill gesture for the day."

"Who's watching the kids?" Tucker asked.

"My grandmother is here for Christmas," Daisy said. "Now tell us what to do, and we'll get it done."

Jena quickly reviewed her clipboard and assigned Tucker's family to the rest of the tasks.

"What about me?" Tucker asked.

"Those lights aren't going to hang themselves, mister."

"You're cute when you're bossy," he returned.

When he started to move away, she stopped him with a hand on his sleeve. "Tucker, your family is wonderful."

"Yeah, I know."

"How can you bear to leave them?"

"It gets harder every single day."

Jena grimaced. "I'm sorry. I know you have a

plan and I'm not trying to make it more difficult to do what you have to do. I'm just very grateful."

He nodded and picked up the box of lights, his expression solemn.

As much as she tried to support his decision to leave, Jena prayed Tucker would wake up and come to his senses. Rebel was his home. This was where he belonged.

Tucker knew the moment Jena entered the room, accompanied by the soft strains of holiday music that filled the event center. He turned as she stepped through the lighted arch they'd created with lights and a trellis at the entrance. Jena's face lit up with delight and a smile touched her lips as she took in the gala before her. She looked like a kid at Christmas.

Mike Ross from Beep Jeep and Finn Hardy spotted Jena, too, and the men crossed the room at the same time from different directions. He couldn't deny he was jealous as they vied for her attention. Jena laughed and smiled at them both.

"Bunch of yahoos," Mitch muttered. "Are you going to just stand there?"

Tucker turned to see Reece and Mitch right next to him. "What is this? An intervention?"

"It ought to be," Reece said.

"Aren't you going to go over there?" Mitch asked.

"Is there a rush?"

"You let one of those guys get the upper hand, and you won't see Jena for the rest of the evening."

"We're cohosting this shindig. I'll see her. Why don't you two meddlers go find your wives? I've got to get this party started."

The band cued Tucker's music and he stepped up to the microphone. "Welcome to Jingle Paws. Dinner begins in thirty minutes. For those of you who are new to Rebel Ranch, your meal has been prepared by Chef Luna Diaz. You're welcome."

Applause erupted across the room.

"Until then, enjoy the music. Be sure to check out the silent auction items in the room to your right. Magnolia Parker can answer your questions on how that process works. And remember… The animals of the Rebel Vet and Rescue could really use your wallets tonight."

This time, along with applause, hoots and whistles went up in the reception hall.

Tucker headed down the steps to where Jena waited for him.

"Hi there," she said.

"Hey." His mouth was dry as he took in the flirty hem of her forest green dress. "Nice dress." He shook his head, disgusted with himself.

"What's wrong?" she asked.

"You look so beautiful I'm having a difficult time stringing together an intelligent sentence."

Jena laughed. "I thought that was a good one.

Thank you." She glanced around. "The reception hall looks good, doesn't it?"

"Better than good. Everyone is impressed. You've really put them in a holiday mood."

"I'm glad. Maybe we'll be featured in *The Weekly Rebel*."

"I wouldn't be surprised."

"I should go check on the silent auction," she said.

"Save me a dance?" Tucker asked.

"Of course."

The music started. When Mike and Finn looked in their direction, Tucker tensed. "Jena. Wait."

She turned toward him. "Hmm?"

"Do you hear that?" He stopped to listen. Thankfully, it was a slow song. "Dancing is starting. I'm claiming that dance now."

"Now? But I have things to do." She glanced around. "Have you seen Dee? Is she having a good time?"

"Jena, Dee is not your responsibility." As he said the words, Tucker realized that he might be very wrong. But right now, the last thing he wanted to discuss was Dee Smith and the potential disaster that lay ahead. He'd been praying about the situation ever since he'd figured out Dee's real identify. All he could conclude was that getting through Jingle Paws came first. Then he'd have to decide if he should talk to Jena.

"Dee doesn't have anyone right now," Jena said. "And I know what that feels like."

"Your responsibilities can wait five minutes. Come on. Dance with me."

"Five minutes, huh? Has anyone mentioned in the last five minutes that you're stubborn?"

"But that's my most endearing quality."

Jena nearly snorted.

He led her to the dance floor and then took her hand and placed it on his shoulder. At first they stumbled, like they couldn't quite get their steps in sync. It was his fault. Finn Hardy stood at the edge of the dance floor watching them with a smile on his face. He was probably a really good dancer.

"Tucker. Stop moving," Jena commanded.

"Say what?"

"Stop moving."

He glanced around, hoping Finn hadn't seen him step on Jena's toes.

She put her hand on his face and turned him toward her. "Focus, Tucker. Look at me."

"I'm looking."

"Dancing is all about trust. You have to trust your partner."

Tucker looked into her eyes and relaxed. "I trust you." That was the easy part. There was no one he trusted more than Jena.

"Okay, the second part is confidence. Fake it."

"Fake it?"

"No one cares how you move. They care about your attitude. You are a terrific dancer. Say it out loud."

"I'm... I'm a terrific dancer," he repeated.

And just like that they began to move smoothly, as though they'd practiced.

"You are, actually," she said. "Have you had lessons or something?"

Tucker laughed. "I actually like to dance. Nothing fancy. A simple box step makes me happy."

"So you're happy right now?"

Tucker laughed again. "I'm very happy." He nodded to the left. "I beat out two other guys who were ready to ask you to dance."

"Is that why you're happy?" She blinked.

"No, I'm happy because the prettiest girl in the room is dancing with me."

Jena released a small breath. "Tucker, we're friends."

"We are. Isn't that a nice place to start?"

"To start?" Her jaw sagged and alarm filled her brown eyes. "You can't say things like that when you know you're leaving in three weeks."

"Jena, I'm being honest. I don't even understand where this is coming from, and you know what? For tonight, just for tonight, I'm not going to think about anything but enjoying your company."

Her face softened and she, too, let down her guard and allowed herself to relax.

For several minutes they swayed to the music. Jena felt good in his arms. Not just good, more than that. When they moved, he got a whiff of coconut. Her shampoo, she'd said. He liked that scent.

The music ended, and he took her hand and bowed. "Thank you."

"You're welcome." Jena blinked.

When a western jig started, Tucker still held her hand. Around them, people were forming a line for an old-fashioned line dance.

"Do you boot scoot?" he asked.

Jena held up a palm and shook her head. "Oh, no, no. You go right ahead." She turned her head. "In fact, here come Mike and Finn. They'll dance with you."

"When pigs fly," he muttered. Instead, he stood near the dance floor enjoying Nolie and Mrs. Tuttle toe-stepping with ease and giggling like schoolgirls.

By the time dinner was over and the silent auction complete, Tucker was ready to put his feet up and loosen his tie. He checked his phone for messages from the veterinary answering service or Mrs. Stewart as he moved past guests who were admiring the Jingle Paws tree and taking ornaments to fill requests.

Jena had likely survived this 'peopling,' as she called it, by staying busy. He scanned the room for her, but she was petite enough to escape notice in this crowd. The good news was that Mike Ross and Finn Hardy hadn't found her, either. They were also looking around.

Then, from the corner of his eye, he saw the side door open and Jena slip outside. He followed.

"Are you running away?" he asked.

"Tucker!" she turned, surprised. "No, I just needed a breather. There are so many people in there."

Tucker stared at her as the moonlight settled around them. In the distance, the cattle moved across the pasture and overhead a breeze rustled the last of the autumn leaves.

Jena shivered.

"Here." Tucker put his jacket around her shoulders.

"Thank you."

"Tucker, do you think I've changed?"

"You're Jena," he returned.

"You didn't answer my question," she murmured.

"You haven't changed, Jena. You're as beautiful on the outside as you are on the inside. No matter what the future holds, I'll always care for you. Nothing can change that."

For a long moment, she simply stared at him as if pondering his words.

When a sudden breeze pulled her hair, blowing it into a beautiful disarray, Jena raised a hand to straighten the pixie cut. "Oh, now it's a mess."

He took her hand and held it. "It looks good."

She leaned toward him. Like dancing, for once it seemed they were in perfect sync.

He leaned toward her and cupped her face in his palm.

And then the door opened and the light from the hall blinded them.

"Nope. You're wrong," Dee said. "She's not out here, Mrs. Parker. I think she's in the kitchen."

"How can you possibly tell? It's so dark," Nolie said. "Dr. Harper, are you out there?" Nolie called. "You're needed in the auction room."

"Be right there, Nolie," Jena said.

Tucker shook his head as the door closed.

"Remind me to fire her and give Dee a raise," he muttered.

Jena laughed and handed him his jacket. "Let's go in before we do something you might regret."

"Me?" He held the door.

"You're the one leaving, Tucker. Not me."

Tucker slipped his jacket on and straightened his tie. He hated it when she was right.

"I better get to the auction room," Jena said.

"Yeah, of course."

He moved over to the Jingle Paw tree and examined the remaining ornaments.

"Dr. Rainbolt, you look so nice."

He turned at Dee's voice. She wore a green dress tonight, too. "Dee, you, too. You look just like…"

"Like Dr. Harper." She finished the sentence for him.

"Yeah. Just like Jena." The words had slipped out of his mouth before he could do anything about it.

She gave a sad, resigned smile. "I could tell that you knew. That day we were doing Christmas decorations in the office. You looked at me and I could tell."

"Why didn't you say something?" he asked.

"What could I say?" She sighed. "Dr. Rainbolt, this hasn't been some sort of master plan of mine. I truly stumbled into this and I'm playing everything by ear. I knew she was here and yes, I came to town. But everything else. Chester in the tree, the job... It just happened."

"Are you going to tell her?"

"Do you think she wants to know? Not all biological parents do." She clasped her hands tightly. "I've done plenty of research and, well, my parents thought going to a counselor was good. So I did when I was in high school."

He didn't know how to respond. For a moment she seemed to be working up the courage to continue.

When Dee looked at him again, there was pain in her eyes. "Having me around might be the last thing she wants. After all, she didn't want me in the first place."

"Whoa. Whoa. Whoa. I know Dr. Harper, and I

do not believe that is true. Not at all." Jena would want to know. But once again, this wasn't his call to make.

"I don't want to burden her." She bit her lip. "Dr. Harper hides it, but this fundraiser is everything. Sometimes I see her staring at the calendar and she looks so sad. I know she's sad about you leaving and worried about the rescue."

He sighed. "Just promise me you won't hurt her."

"I care a lot about her. I would never do that." She looked at him. "I don't want either one of us to hurt her." Dee stared at him. "You really care for Dr. Harper."

"Jena and I are best friends, Dee."

"No. It's more than that."

Tucker didn't answer. How could he explain how he felt about Jena to an eighteen-year-old? He couldn't even explain it satisfactorily to himself.

"You know, Dr. Rainbolt, sometimes when we're in the middle of the storm, we can't see the right direction. Dr. Harper is your direction."

"Kiddo, you're like an eighty-year-old in the body of an eighteen-year-old. How did you get to be so wise?"

"My mother. My adoptive mother, I mean. And good genes, I guess."

"I guess."

"Are we good, Dr. Rainbolt?" Dee asked. "You and me?"

"We are, Dee, but you have to tell her as soon as you can. Keeping secrets never ends well."

She nodded and turned away.

Tucker looked across the room to where Jena stood directing volunteers. He couldn't help the sense of foreboding that raced over him. All he could do was be there when Jena needed a friend and hope that would be enough.

Chapter Nine

"The rescue is a liability and a financial drain, Dr. Harper. We can't approve a loan for the building unless you are willing to consider separating yourself from the rescue."

"But it's not my rescue. It's a nonprofit. All the appropriate paperwork has been filed."

"Still, you are listed as the registered agent. All liability falls upon you. The bank would be much more inclined to consider your request if your name was not on the rescue's filing paperwork."

She stared at the man behind the desk. "You want me to cut off my left arm to save my right?"

"That seems a touch overly dramatic."

"Not to me, it doesn't." She stood. "Thank you for your time. Mr. Lee."

"Take some time to think about it, Dr. Harper. Our terms are very reasonable. Read through the paperwork."

She shook her head. "No, thank you. The rescue and the clinic are a package deal. I can't do what you suggest."

"Can't or won't? Sometimes fiscally sound decisions can be painful," he said with a cheerful grin.

"Merry Christmas, Mr. Lee. I'll give your regards to all the kittens and puppies at the rescue."

Jena strode down the street, trying to walk off her anger. She kicked at a small bank of snow and grumbled.

Passing the rescue, Jena stopped and looked in the window. The staff typically rotated animals in the front-window kennel to attract people walking down Rebel Avenue. Today, two bonded kittens wrestled, rolling around on a sheepskin blanket.

A young woman stopped outside the window and stared. "Oh, aren't they precious?" she asked to no one in particular.

Jena couldn't help but answer. "They are and the nice thing about two is they keep each other company."

"Still, it's quite a commitment."

"Absolutely. A lifetime commitment. Pets are your family. They provide unconditional love and, in return, all they ask is that you love them. Forever."

The woman looked from Jena to the window, her eyes round.

"Why don't you go in and hold them. They'd

love that. You don't have to decide today. Just give them some love. Maybe you'd like to be a volunteer. Kitten cuddlers are always in high demand."

"Why, I think I'll do that. Thank you." She pulled open the door to the rescue and walked in.

Jena's shoulders sagged and the anger that had made her rigid as she walked down the street dissipated. Mr. Lee was clueless. Never, ever would she abandon the rescue.

She opened the front door to the clinic and looked around the waiting room. A twelve-year-old beagle waited for her.

"Good afternoon, Mrs. Brown. How's Sigmund Freud?"

"Better," the elderly woman said.

"Good. We'll draw his blood work again today. Don't you worry. If he continues to respond to treatment, I feel confident that he'll be recovered in time for Christmas."

"Thank you, Dr. Harper."

Jena hung up her coat and stopped at the desk to talk to Nolie. "Could you please have Pilar draw Siggie's blood work before the appointment?"

"Yes, ma'am." Nolie looked at Jena. "Are you—"

"Do not ask me if I'm okay. I am fine."

Jena put on a happy face for her back-to-back appointments. By 4:00 p.m., she was done for the day. She walked to her office, sank into her chair and began a silent prayer. There had to be a way to save the building.

"Jena?"

"I'm fine, Tucker." She rubbed her forehead and didn't look up.

"Of course you are."

She hadn't had a minute to even think about Tucker or the outrageous things he'd said at the dinner Friday. Or even consider that almost-kiss. Saturday had been a blur of business as Jingle Paws continued, and Sunday was cleanup. Monday was nearly over, and her thoughts were scrambled and she was exhausted.

"Did you need something?" she asked.

"How did the bank appointment go?"

"How did you know that was today?" This time she did look up.

"I was heading out of the post office when you were going into the bank."

"Everything is just…" She stopped when he leveled her with a look that said *don't fool me.* "It went terrible. They'll only consider me for the loan if I disaffiliate from the rescue. That's not an option. Ever."

"I agree with you." He took a deep breath. "I'm sorry, Jena."

"There's more. That rental space? They don't want animals." Jena shook her head and stood. "I'm not sure how this day can get worse. I'm going to head on home." She circled her desk and went out to the reception area to grab her coat.

"Are you Jena Harper?"

Jena turned in time to see a man she didn't recognize at the front desk.

Nolie looked up from her computer. "No. That's Dr. Harper."

The man turned to Jena, anguish in his eyes. "You've taken my daughter away from me. Why? You had your chance. You gave her up."

"Excuse me. Who are you?" Jena asked. Even as she asked, she knew. Maybe she'd known all along.

"Frank Smith. Dee's—"

"Dee's father." Jena's heart raced as she said the words. She fought to catch her breath.

Tucker was beside her in a moment. "Mr. Smith. I'm Dr. Rainbolt. Let's go into my office to talk."

"Where's Dee?" Jena asked Nolie as Tucker led Dee's father down the hall.

"She's off today." The receptionist's face was ashen.

"It's okay, Nolie. Everything is going to be fine."

Jena pushed the glass door open and stepped outside. When her cell phone rang, she pulled it from her pocket. *Tucker*.

"Jena, where are you?"

"I'm going to talk to Dee."

"Okay. Good idea. Dee's father is okay. He's just upset, poor guy. I explained that you didn't know."

"Thanks, Tucker." Her teeth chattered, and she realized that she'd forgotten her coat.

"You'll call me if you need me?" he asked.

"I will." She shoved the phone in her pocket. The only thing she needed was answers.

Her head continued to spin with questions as she walked around the block to the entrance door to the apartment above the clinic and pressed the buzzer. The sound of feet pounding down the stairs grew louder until the door opened without ceremony.

"Did you look through the peephole?" Jena asked. "You should always check to see who's at the door first."

Dee's eyes rounded with surprise at Jena's words. "I'm sorry. I didn't think…"

Jena sighed as she realized the irony of the situation. Here she was, acting like…acting like Dee's mother or something. She caught her breath. "Can we talk?"

Dee nodded and licked her lips as if she knew exactly what was coming.

Jena followed her upstairs to the little apartment where Chester sat in the window watching the world. She took a calming breath.

"You're my daughter." *My daughter.* The words

Jena never expected to say slipped from her lips, both comforting and confusing her.

Dee's blue ponytail bobbed. "Uh-huh."

"Why didn't you tell me?"

"It all sort of happened so fast. I didn't know how to tell you. I didn't expect to find you. Then when I did, I wasn't sure you wanted to be found."

"How did you find me?"

"My mom."

"Your mom?" Of course. Jena's great-aunt had the information about Dee's parents and never shared it with Jena. Dee's parents had the same information.

"Before she died, she gave me your name and told me you're a vet. I guess she looked you up. She suggested that when I was ready, I should find you." Dee wrung her hands together. "I didn't have a clue about protocol, so I thought I'd drive through town." She swallowed. "Then I saw the ad when I was at the diner. I really did need a job."

Jena covered her mouth with her hands, trying desperately to take it all in. She couldn't help but look at Dee and try to put all the pieces of the last eighteen years together in her head. The baby she'd handed over to the nurse that day, that brown-eyed baby, had grown up. This young woman was that baby. Her baby.

The room was silent, the only sound was an occasional car passing by on Oak Road.

"Are you mad?"

"Mad? No. I don't know what I am. But mad isn't on the radar."

"You were fifteen?" Dee asked.

"Yes." A single word that had shamed her all these years, suddenly lost a tiny bit of its power. "Sixteen when you were born."

"So I was definitely a mistake."

"I don't believe that. Not for a single minute." She met Dee's gaze.

Dee offered a smile and relaxed a bit. "Do I look like you?"

"I have no idea. I'm still pretty much in shock."

"What about family? Do I have any other family?" Dee asked as though hungry for information.

Jena knew that feeling. The need to know. It remained unquenched in her for eighteen years.

"It's just me," Jena said. My parents, your biological grandparents, are in Tulsa, but they disowned me because I got pregnant."

"Disowned. People do that?"

"Sadly, yes." She looked at Dee. "What's going on with you and your father?"

"He wants me in college, though we cannot afford it after my mom's medical bills." She paused. "And he didn't want me to find you."

"I fully support him on the first." Jena chewed her lip for a moment.

"And the second?"

"I'm glad you're here." Jena hesitated, her stomach in knots. "But I'm going to need some time to process this."

"Sure, I get that." Dee bit her lip. "Do I still have a job?"

"Of course."

Dee nodded. "This is sort of surreal, isn't it?"

"Very. But in a good way. As for the rest, we'll figure it out as we go." Jena offered a smile. "Does that work for you?"

"Therefore, do not worry about tomorrow, for tomorrow will worry about itself. Each day has enough trouble of its own," Dee said.

"Exactly."

"What do we do next?" Dee asked.

"I feel like maybe I should hug you or shake your hand or something."

"A hug would be good." Dee reached out to embrace her.

The warmth of the connection filled Jena's heart with a crushing wave of emotion. She'd waited eighteen years for this moment, believing it would never come. She swallowed and blinked as fast as she could to stop the tears, because she knew once she started, she'd never be able to stop.

"Dr. Harper, how did you find out?" Dee asked.

"Your father."

Dee's eyes grew wide and she released a stuttered breath. "Oh, no."

"He's in the clinic. In Dr. Rainbolt's office."

"Is he mad?"

"Dee, mad isn't anywhere in this situation. He's worried and upset. I want you to make things right with him. Go home to Tulsa. Take Chester. Consider yourself on vacation until after Christmas. Your father deserves to have his daughter with him for Christmas." Jena peered at Dee. "Do you understand?"

Dee nodded. "Um, could I ask a question?"

"Sure."

"What should I call you?"

Jena raised her palms and smiled. For the first time today, she wanted to laugh with joy. "I don't have a clue."

Tucker walked back and forth outside of Jena's door, his boots making imprints in the dusting of snow, as he debated his options. He didn't want to bother her, but he couldn't leave her to deal with this alone. A part of him still battled with whether he was wrong not to tell her about Dee when he realized the truth.

Taking a deep breath, he turned and knocked at the door.

Jena opened it. She looked up at him with a forlorn expression, like one of the puppies in the rescue front window. His heart ached for her.

"Come on in, Tucker."

"How can I help?" He shook the snow off his boots on her doormat and stepped into the warm house. Ernie whined and rubbed her head on Tucker's leg.

"There's not a thing you can do to help me. I did this to myself."

Tucker ran a hand over his face. This was a worst-case scenario and he didn't have a fix or even the right words to comfort her.

"Dee is my daughter. How could I not have known my own daughter?" She went to the couch and plopped down, grabbing a throw pillow and clutching it to her chest.

"You said you never had any information. Why are you blaming yourself?"

"I should have known. I should have known. Mothers know those things."

"Being a mother isn't a wholly biological thing, Jena. You know that. You adopt animals into homes for a living and then care for those animals. Animals who become fur-babies to people for the rest of both of their lives." He paused, still waging an internal war about telling her the truth.

"Jena, I need you to know that Dee told me she was your daughter. I had pretty much figured it out already, and she confirmed my thoughts at the Jingle Paws dinner."

A small gasp slipped from her mouth and she stared at him, stunned. "Why didn't you tell me?"

He sat down on the couch. "It was near the end of the evening. There was no way I could tell you then. Dee assured me that she planned to tell you herself." He hesitated again. "Jena, you should also know that Dee was very concerned that you might not want to know."

"Oh, that poor girl," she said with a groan. "Look how many lives I've messed up with my mistakes."

"Stop being so hard on yourself. You haven't messed up anything, and there is no way you could have known."

"None of this would have happened if I had an iota of maternal instinct."

"Stop saying that, will you? Maternal instinct has nothing to do with it. I can see you and Dee next to each other. See your gestures. See how you laugh the same, think the same. You can't possibly have that objective view."

Jena's face crumpled and she hid behind her hands.

"Oh, Jena." He put his arms around her and held her tightly, offering a silent prayer of comfort. After a few minutes she relaxed against his chest, and he felt silent tears drop on his hand.

Tucker let her cry. Let her cry for all the misery of her past. For the loss of parents who had abandoned her. For everything.

He wished in that moment that he could hold her forever.

After a while she took a long shuddering breath and pulled away from him. "You should go. I'm keeping you from your children."

"It's fine. I gave Mrs. Stewart a heads-up."

She sniffled and wiped her eyes with the sleeve of her sweatshirt. "There's nothing you can do, Tucker. I'll have a pity party and then pick myself up and try to figure out what's next."

"What is next?"

"Well, the good news is that I ran the numbers for the fundraiser. We raised enough money to keep the rescue afloat for another year. The bad news is we still don't have a building."

"So we'll figure it out. That's what we do, right? Team Jena and Tucker."

A tiny smile lifted the corners of her mouth. "Put away your pom-poms. I think this one may be an overreach for our skill set."

"I don't believe that." He looked around when he heard a rumbling noise. "What was that?"

"My stomach." Her smile was now touched with embarrassment.

"When was the last time you ate?"

"I don't know. I had a donut in the break room before I went to the bank."

"Let me make you something to eat."

"You?"

"Don't look at me like that." Did everyone think he was just a pretty face? "I told you that I can cook. Mitch made sure all of us were prepared to live on our own. I'm only limited by your refrigerator."

"I have eggs and bacon."

"Do you have bread?"

Jena raised her shoulders. "Bagels in the freezer."

"Cheese?"

"There's some brie in the back of the fridge."

"Then we have dinner." He held out his hand and pulled her to her feet. "Let's go."

She screwed up her face and followed him to the kitchen. "You do not have to make me dinner. I am perfectly capable of doing it on my own."

"So we do it together. I'm hungry, too. We'll eat and then try to fix this situation."

"There's nothing to fix. Dee is home with her father for Christmas. When she comes back, I'll figure out how to be a mother to an eighteen-year-old woman."

"And the building?"

"All I want to do about that is moan and groan. Your job is to listen and nod and cluck. That's what best friends do."

"Naw, that's what girlfriends do. I'm not your girlfriend." He raised his brows. "I'm your guy friend."

Her guy friend with lousy timing who was beginning to realize that he wanted to be much more than a friend.

"It may be time for a reality check," Jena said. "There is no solution."

"That we know of."

Jena snorted. "You just can't help it, can you?" She shook her head. "I don't even get it. Your mother died, your dad ran away and you've had more loss in the last five or six years than I can imagine. Why are you smiling?"

"What's the alternative? And by the way, are we assigning points to our painful life moments? You're not exactly the poster child for a stellar childhood either, yet I don't see you throwing in the towel." He grabbed the eggs from the fridge. "We're a lot alike, you and I."

"Point taken. So what's your secret, Tucker?"

"Every time I feel overwhelmed by life, the Lord pins back my ears and says the same thing And I don't mean in an audible voice. I mean in my gut. 'Either you trust me or you don't, Tucker. Either you're with me or you walk away.'"

Jena released a breath. "Yes, exactly. I whine a little while and then I become resolute and focused as I carry on."

"That, my friend, is faith. The good fight. You and I have faith."

"I probably could eliminate the middle man and go straight to faith."

Tucker smiled. "We're human. We moan a little. It's normal."

In the corner Ernie barked as if to agree. Then she continued to kill her favorite toy, looking their way on occasion if she thought food might appear.

"So here we are." He resisted the urge to put his arms around her again. They were so much alike and it had taken him way too long to understand that Jena was the only person in the world who understood him the way he understood her. Only now it might be too late to explore the possibilities that came with this revelation.

"Here we are," Jena agreed.

Tucker opened the freezer and pulled out a plastic bag. He grimaced as he examined the contents. "What is this?"

"Homemade dog biscuits. What does it look like?"

"I'm not sure."

Ernie barked and jumped up, placing her paws on Tucker's hip.

"Now that she's seen them, we have to defrost the biscuits," Jena said.

Tucker laughed. "She's a dog, Jena. You do not have to do what a dog tells you to do."

"Tell her that."

"Can you find those bagels?" He opened the fridge once more. "I don't see your hot sauce."

"Hot sauce? You're making eggs."

"Exactly."

"It's between the salsa and the barbeque sauce, right where it should be."

"Frying pan?"

Jena pulled the bagels from the freezer and then opened a cupboard. She grabbed a bowl and a frying pan.

"Thank you." Tucker put the bacon in the frying pan, and soon the savory scent filled the kitchen. Once they were crisp, he placed them on a paper towel and then cracked the eggs into a bowl and whipped them up.

"Are you making scrambled eggs?"

"No. An omelet. We can split it."

"I like that. I can't make omelets."

"Can you put the bagels in the toaster?"

"I can do that."

They worked together silently for a few minutes. Teamwork. Like they had for seven years in the clinic, except now it was personal, and he liked that. Liked being with Jena outside of the building in downtown Rebel that had defined their relationship for so many years.

When they sat down to eat, Tucker took her hand. "Lord, thank You for this food and bless it to our bodies, and can You give us a clue how to fix the building problem? Amen."

Jena opened her eyes and looked at him flatly. "You really are incorrigible."

"What? I told you. I don't leave for another three weeks. I'm still the co-owner of Rebel Vet until we sign the paperwork. I'm obligated to care about the rescue and the building."

Tucker's gaze wandered to Jena as they silently ate. This was the way it should be. Comfortable silence. He'd missed that over the years.

When he finished, he stood with his dish and reached for Jena's empty plate, as well. "I'll wash."

"Tell you what, Tucker, you walk Ernie and I'll do the dishes."

When he came back from his walk, Jena was asleep on the couch.

"Shh, girl, be quiet. Let her sleep." Tucker covered Jena with a quilt and pressed a kiss to her forehead. "We're going to figure this out, Jena. I promise."

Tucker closed the door carefully and left her house. He sat in his truck and started the engine, letting the heater warm the space. Then he called Reece. "I want to discuss a proposition with you."

"I'm listening."

"I want to sell part of my inheritance, my shares in Rebel Ranch."

"Tucker, what's going on?"

"I want to buy the clinic and rescue building."

"We've already had this discussion. You're leaving Rebel."

"This is what I want. Call it my Christmas present. You can make the others agree, Reece. Mitch will go along if you agree, and Kate, well, she's already on my side."

"I'll have to call our attorney in Tulsa and try to get in before he takes off for the holidays."

"Can you make it happen?"

"For you, little brother? Yeah, I'll do it." He paused. "I hope Jena knows how you feel about her."

Tucker jerked back at the words. "This isn't about Jena. It's about the animals."

"I know you care about the animals. But you're doing this for Jena."

"That's not true."

"You've fallen for your best friend, Tucker. I may not be the Rainbolt with the fancy college degree, but I can see the truth pretty clearly, and brother, you've fallen. Hard."

"No." Tucker's head began to spin as he tried to wrap his thoughts around what Reece said. He cared for Jena plenty, and yeah, those feelings were growing. He'd readily admit that after the last few days.

But love? How could he have made the leap to love? Tucker froze as the revelation barreled into him.

"Yeah. The part I can't figure is why you're leaving town if everything you ever wanted is here. In Rebel."

"I…"

"Tucker, trust me. I've been there, and boy have I done that. I lost years of time I could have spent with my wife and daughter because I didn't want to see what was right in front of me."

"Sure, okay, I care for Jena."

The windshield wipers swished back and forth, whispering to him.

You love Jena.

He'd been looking for change. Not love. Never in a million years would he think that love would find him a second time.

"That admission will get you one building."

"What did you say?" Tucker checked the volume on his phone.

"Rebel Ranch will buy that building. I won't let you sell your heritage. I can't do that. It goes against everything that I believe in. You know that."

"Did you just say Rebel Ranch will buy the building?"

"I have to get Mitch and Kate's approval, and they're going to have to know what's going on."

"What's going on?"

"Tuck, I thought we already established what's going on. You're going to have to try to keep up, man."

"Wait a minute. I thought you said that Rebel Ranch can't afford to buy the building."

"No, I said that it wasn't a sound investment for the ranch. Our finances are just fine and if you ever took the time to look at the reports I send you from the accountant each month, you'd know we can afford to buy the building. My emphasis was on the fact that it didn't make sense to buy the building if you were leaving town."

"I'm still leaving town."

"Not likely. And while I have your attention, I spoke with Mitch this morning. He said to remind you that you need to call Professor Leonard at OSU back."

"So he did finesse that job offer?"

"You'll have to talk to Mitch."

"You know, you're starting to annoy me."

Reece laughed. "Welcome to my world."

Tucker began to backpedal. "Maybe I should sleep on the whole building idea." He rubbed his jaw. "I've still got a week or so to come up with a better idea."

"Doesn't get any better than family. I buy the building, and Rebel Vet and Rescue stays put. They pay rent to the best-looking landlord in town."

Tucker laughed. "Now you're delusional."

"You want my advice?" Reece asked.

"Absolutely not."

"You're going to get it anyhow. Go to Texas, explain why you can't take the position. You don't want to burn bridges. Thank them. Then let Finn take over the equine clinic."

"Why would I do that?"

"You have a perfect setup here. A job offer, a woman you love. Family." Reece paused. "You've been breaking your back for years running from your pain. I know you think you're hiding it, but you can't hide it from me and Mitch. We've walked the same road."

Tucker didn't know what to say. There it was. The truth poking him in the eye.

"You still there?" Reece asked.

"Yes," he mumbled.

"Good. Because now that I have doled out brotherly advice, I have to go. This has been fun, but I've got a meeting in Oklahoma City tomorrow."

"Hey, Reece."

"Yeah?"

"Thanks. I mean it."

"Aw, don't go all sappy on me or I'll rescind the offer."

Tucker disconnected the call and sat back in the seat. He pulled off his hat and ran a hand through his hair. Somehow his life had been turned upside down today. The truth of the last month and a half settled over him and he realized that he had a lot of undoing of plans already in place to do. When he was done, he'd talk to Jena about what came next.

Chapter Ten

❧

"We're home." Tucker got out of his truck and released Hazel and Ginger from their car seats.

The twins sprung from the vehicle, clutching their preschool drawings and chattering as they walked up the cobblestone path to the house.

"Daddy, we play in yard?" Ginger asked.

He glanced around, knowing his parcel of land on Rebel Guest Ranch was safe and secure and even boasted a five-foot cedar fence that surrounded the back of the property. Yet, it was his routine to evaluate every situation from a worst-case scenario point of view.

"Daddy?" Hazel called, her voice laced with impatience.

"Yes, you may. Just until I unload the truck." He paused. "Do not take your coats off." As usual, he tried to stay one step ahead of their game, often failing at that, too.

"Yes, Daddy," they echoed in unison.

As they disappeared around the house, he unloaded a bag of groceries from the front seat of his vehicle. For a moment, he stood evaluating the little house. It held a lot of memories. Maybe too many. If everything went as planned, things were about to change. Leaving this house and the bittersweet memories was probably a good idea. It was the only way he could move forward.

He turned in time to see a huge black truck slow down and stop in the gravel road in front of his house.

Reece got out of the pickup and yawned.

"Tired?" Tucker asked. "Didn't see you when I was out at the clinic this morning."

"Good to know you're monitoring my activities. Where were you at three a.m.?"

"Excuse me?"

"My daughter was up half the night with a stomach bug."

"Hope she's feeling better, but stand back." Tucker held up a hand. "Last thing I need is germs. I'm leaving for Dallas in a few hours."

"Take it easy, I'm just here to drop off a care package from Luna."

"Luna?" Tucker perked up. There was nothing like Luna Diaz's care packages.

"What is it?"

"Enchilada casserole. Had a party of ranch guests cancel because of the weather. Apparently, it's snowing in Denver. Anyhow, she ended up with extras."

"I can't believe I'm saying this, but maybe you should take it," Tucker said. "You're the one short on sleep."

Reece scoffed. "I got mine first."

"I figured. Here we go again. Tucker William Rainbolt, the hand-me-down brother. Third in line."

Reece was unmoved. "That worked when you were five. Not so much when you're standing nose-to-nose with me."

Tucker grinned. He liked playing the little bro card. Sometimes it came in handy.

"Tell Luna thank you. This is perfect timing. I forgot to defrost something for lunch and Jena is on her way over."

"I'll tell her." Reece offered a benevolent smile. "So I imagine things are going well between you and Jena?"

"I've spent the last forty-eight hours trying to undo everything I set in motion for Texas."

"You haven't talked to her?"

"Soon. I told you I leave for Texas tonight. Jena is going to watch the girls overnight. Mrs. Stewart is gone until tomorrow morning."

"This is unbelievable. You need some help getting your life in order?"

"You and Mitch need to keep your boots out of my business."

"Next week is Christmas. We'd like to see everything settled by then."

"We?" Tucker scoffed. "I'm seriously thinking about ratting you two out to Daisy and Claire."

Reece raised his palms. "All right, we'll back off, but you best not mess this up."

"I won't."

"So why were you staring so hard at the house when I pulled up?"

"I'm thinking maybe letting Kate have the place would be a good idea."

Reece chuckled. "You haven't told Jena you love her and already you're planning to expand your family. I believe they call that putting the cart before the horse."

"You know, I don't know why I talk to you. You're as annoying as Mitch."

"I'll try harder."

Tucker glanced at his watch.

"Am I keeping you from something?"

"I told you Jena is on her way over." He looked toward the house. "And the girls have been in the backyard unsupervised for four minutes."

"Four minutes, huh?"

"That's enough time for them to tunnel under the fence and be halfway to Okmulgee. Are you going to give me that casserole or talk all day?"

Reece grabbed the glass casserole dish and handed it to Tucker. "Enjoy."

"Reece, you can't tell anyone about the building yet."

"Does she know you're not moving to Texas?"

"No. I'm working up to it."

"She doesn't know you love her, or about the building or Texas?"

"That's right and if you keep your mouth shut nothing will go wrong."

"Nothing will go wrong?" Reece started laughing. "That's the spirit. And someday you, too, will laugh about this."

Barely fifteen minutes later, Jena was on his stoop. Tucker opened the door and urged her inside.

"Quick," he said. "Before the zoo gets out."

Jena laughed, her voice warm with delight. "Sounds like my house." Stepping into his foyer, she placed a small duffel on the ground and tossed her coat on top of it.

She was so pretty, and he longed to have the right to tell her so as often as possible and to take her in his arms and kiss her as often as possible, too.

"You're staring."

"Oh, sorry."

Maybe they should talk now. After his conversation with Reece, he found himself second-guessing his decision not to tell her about everything first. No. He had a plan and he'd stick to it. Today was Wednesday. He'd be back to work on Friday. Then he'd tell her everything. Yeah, it was a good plan. It was his Christmas present to Jena. And he only prayed everything worked out in real time the way it had in his head.

"What are you thinking about so hard?" Jena asked.

"Nothing. Sorry. I'm distracted with this trip."

"I don't want to talk about Texas," she said. "I'm here for food and my girls. I'm going to pretend Texas doesn't exist."

Tucker smiled at her words.

She walked toward the kitchen, sniffing with appreciation. "I smell cheese. What did you make? I demand to be led to whatever it is, immediately."

"First, I have to tell you something. It's a good news, bad news thing."

"Go ahead. I'm ready."

"Lunch is an enchilada casserole from Luna Diaz."

"Clearly that's the good news. And the bad news?"

"My flight times changed and I have to leave as soon as we eat."

"Not a problem."

"You're sure?"

"Tucker, I'm just delighted you're letting me spend time with them. You're going to be in Texas soon and I'm going to miss them." Jena glanced around the living room. "Where are they? It's awfully quiet around here."

"Hazel. Ginger. Time to eat."

There was no response, but he heard chatter.

He strode down the hall and then stopped to pinpoint the location of the chatter. His office.

"Uh-oh. This can't be good," Jena murmured.

Tucker opened the door slowly. Ginger and Hazel sat on the floor with red and blue pens drawing on each other's arms and legs.

"What are you doing?" Tucker barely got the words out, he was so flabbergasted.

"Hi, Daddy," Ginger said with a grin. "We draw pictures."

"Why? We have plenty of paper."

Hazel straightened her shirt and stood.

"You aren't supposed to draw on your skin," he said. In a quick swoop he took the pens from their hands.

Jena snickered, and he shot her a glance. "And you aren't supposed to laugh."

"I can't help it," she whispered back.

"Ginger told me to," Hazel said. The big blue eyes were moist with tears as she peeked at him through the caramel locks that had fallen from her barrette.

Tucker knelt down and took his daughter's hand, tucking her hair behind her ear. "I love you just the way you are. Let's not draw on your skin again. Okay?"

"Okay, Daddy," Hazel said solemnly.

Ginger stood and moved to put her arms around Hazel. "I sorry."

"You aren't in trouble," Tucker said. "But we have to hurry. Aunty Jena is here for lunch and I leave soon."

Hazel looked up. "Aunty Jena!"

Ginger whirled around. "Aunty Jena!"

"Hello, my darlings." Jena turned to Tucker. "We'll need washcloths and shaving cream."

"Shaving cream?"

"It's basically just soap, but it's more fun and less drying than rubbing alcohol."

"Shaving cream? How do you know this?"

She smiled. "Let's file that under a discussion for another day."

Twenty minutes later, with the girls all cleaned up, Tucker grabbed the handle of his carry-on bag and wheeled it toward the door. "I apologize. That totally did not go as planned. I thought we'd have lunch and talk before I left."

"It's fine."

"Did I tell you that Mrs. Stewart will be back by nine tomorrow morning?"

"Five times."

"What?"

"You told me that five times."

"Aunty Jena." Hazel's voice rang out.

"Coming, sweetie."

"Do you want me to…?" When Tucker moved

forward, Jena quickly side-stepped and put her hand on his chest.

"If you pop your head in the kitchen, they'll want another round of goodbyes."

"You're right. I don't know how you figured that out, but you're right." He stood in the same spot, wanting to leave but unable to move.

He didn't want to leave her or the twins. He longed to sit down at the table and eat Luna's casserole and pretend they were a family.

Tucker released a breath, continuing to pray that everything was going to work out. He'd be back here in a few days and they'd have the best Christmas ever.

"Go, Tucker," Jena said softly. "I'll text you updates."

"Yeah. Yeah. Please do that." He took a deep breath. "I feel terrible. I haven't even asked you if you're doing okay. Have you heard from Dee?"

"I'm fine. We'll catch up when you get back."

Still, he didn't move. He stared at her mouth, distracted.

"Tucker?"

"Hmm?"

When he met Jena's gaze, a small smile lifted her lips as she reached around him and opened the door. "It's time."

He nodded and turned, as he silently vowed that he was never going to leave home overnight again.

* * *

"Dr. Harper. Merry Christmas."

Jena looked up from her desk. "Charlie! How nice to see you."

"What do you have there?"

She knew exactly what it was, but she liked to humor Charlie. He'd been gifting the office a fruitcake each year as a thank you for being such good tenants. Jena was the only person in the office who actually liked fruitcake, which worked well for her, except Charlie's wife made fruitcakes the size of an Oklahoma bison. Jena had seven years of leftover fruitcake in her freezer.

Still, it was tradition, and this would be the last year, because in approximately two weeks, he wouldn't be their landlord. Happy Pets would own the building. She did her best not to let him see her distress as that information weighed down her holiday spirit.

"Hard to believe this is the last year, right?" He offered her the round, plaid tin. "If I was a sentimental man, I might shed a tear."

"Oh, Charlie, we're going to miss you. But you'll still come by with your cats."

"I guess the free exams are out the window."

"I guess." She didn't have the heart to tell him that Happy Pets wasn't likely to comp free veterinary exams.

"I bet you're excited," he said.

"Christmas is coming right up," she returned.

"No, I mean about the building."

Jena snapped to attention at his words. "What about the building?"

Charlie's eyes widened. "Uh-oh, maybe I wasn't supposed to say anything. This was probably a Christmas present. My wife is going to be very unhappy if I spoiled the surprise."

"What surprise?"

"Well, now I can't very well tell you, can I?" Panic filled his eyes, and he glanced around. "Is Dr. Rainbolt here?"

"He's with a patient."

"Maybe I should wait." He swallowed hard and glanced at the thick envelope in his hands. "Maybe not. I just got back from the attorney's office. Why don't you give this to Dr. Rainbolt and have him call me?" He shook his head. "Or not."

"Charlie? What's going on?"

"Ask Dr. Rainbolt." He turned and started to go. "Merry Christmas, Dr. Harper. And try to remember that it's the thought that counts."

Jena stepped into the hallway and looked around. Things were quiet. Everyone had left for the Christmas holiday but her and Tucker and Nolie. Tomorrow was their last day in the office for a week. The office would be closed tomorrow at 3:00 p.m. and stay closed except for emergencies for the entire week of Christmas.

"Nolie?" Jena looked around the desk and

found a note taped to the computer that read, *Gone to bank.*

A few minutes later Tucker stepped out of an exam room with Ramon Gallegos and a German shepherd puppy. "We'll see you two after the holidays for vaccinations," Tucker said.

Ramon looked up as they approached the desk. "Dr. Harper, I haven't had a chance to thank you for all you did."

"Things are going well?"

"Very well. Pilar and I and the boys are spending the holidays together."

"I'm so happy for you. Merry Christmas, Ramon."

"Thanks. You, too." He stopped. "I guess I'll be seeing you for the vaccinations after the holidays. I just heard that Dr. Rainbolt is leaving us."

"Yes. That's correct."

"That's too bad. You're going to miss him, I'm sure."

When Tucker offered her a wink, she willed her pulse to slow down.

"We're all going to miss him," Jena said.

The front door closed and Tucker grinned at her like a man who had the world by the tail. "Have I thanked you for babysitting the girls?"

"You have."

"It sure is good to be home," he said. "Want to grab one of those eggnog lattes at the diner?"

"Maybe later…" Though she suspected that if she was right, she might be too mad for lattes.

"Are you okay?" he asked.

Silence stretched between them like the still before the storm. Jena reminded herself to stay calm and not jump to judgment regarding Charlie's bumbling outburst about the building.

"I'm just fine. Do you have a minute?" she asked.

"Sure. My office or yours?"

"You don't fit in my office. I'll meet you in yours. I need to grab something first."

Tucker was at his desk looking at charts when Jena handed him the envelope from Charlie. "What's this?" he asked.

"A Christmas present from Charlie."

"Charlie was here?"

"He made a hasty departure when he realized that he'd put his snowshoes in his mouth. But he didn't quite explain what was going on. Maybe you'd like to."

Tucker narrowed his eyes and had the good grace to look nervous. "Did you look at the paperwork?"

"No. I was afraid to." She shook her head. "What did you do, Tucker?"

"I bought the building. Technically, Rebel Ranch bought the building." He raised his palms. "There it is."

"I told you that I could do this myself."

"Fine. Rebel Ranch owns the building and you can buy it from us when you're able."

Jena crossed her arms and paced in front of his desk as thoughts raced through her head. Didn't he believe she was capable of negotiating with Reece on her own? Did Tucker think their friendship…or whatever their new footing was, was about him taking care of her?

They were equals and she had only recently embraced her worth. She wasn't going to go back to the person she was just a few months ago.

"We talked about this already," she said slowly. "I made my opinion clear, and you knew this was the last thing I wanted."

"So you'd rather lose it all than let me help you with the clinic that we both love more than anything?"

"That's not it. I need to prove to myself that I can stand on my own two feet without you. You've run the show for seven years. You're leaving. I need to prove to myself that I can do the job."

"This really isn't about you, Jena. It's about those animals. You said so yourself. The trauma of moving them in the middle of winter. And where to?"

"That's not fair. You know how much effort I've put into this. I'm barely sleeping, trying to find a way to save what we both worked so hard to build."

"Jena, we were running out of time. Happy

Pets wanted that building when our lease runs out on January first."

"It was my job to beg Reece to buy the building, if that's what it came down to. My job to find a solution to the problem."

"Rebel Ranch bought the building. Not Reece."

"You aren't listening to me. You're my friend. You care for me. I get that. But it doesn't change the fact that you went behind my back and did the very thing I asked you not to do. I don't know if I can forgive you for this."

"I had a very good reason and if you'll give me a chance, I can tell you about it."

"No. It doesn't matter how you spin this. You broke your promise. That's pretty much all I need to know."

He broke her promise and her heart, all in the same day.

Chapter Eleven

"Let me get this straight," Nolie said. "You're mad at him for taking care of the building problem?"

Jena nearly dropped the cup in her hand. She whirled away from the coffee maker, almost toppling over the decorative Christmas tree on the table. "How did you know that?"

"I have superpowers."

"You eavesdropped!"

Nolie stepped into the break room and gave an unapologetic shrug. "Potato. Potahto."

"Look, Nolie, Tucker is leaving us. I'm the boss." She put her cup down as the receptionist approached with a steely determination in her stride. "It's no longer his place to take care of my problems," Jena continued. When Nolie put her hands on her hips, she knew that she was in trouble.

"Excuse me for saying so, Dr. Harper, but

there's more at stake here than just you. If this building was sold to Happy Pets, we'd all be out of a job. Yes, I could reapply somewhere else, but what are the chances that a woman of a certain age would be able to get a job and not have to go back to minimum wage? Slim to none. I can tell you that!"

Okay, she hadn't even thought about the employees. Jena did a mental forehead slap. What kind of horrible boss did that make her? She opened her mouth to respond, but Nolie was on a roll.

"Then there's the rescue. What would happen to the animals?" Nolie clucked her tongue. "Rescues aren't big business. Why, if it wasn't for Jingle Paws, you might be closing your doors anyhow. Am I right?"

Jena narrowed her gaze. "How do you know all this?"

"I run the office. Every piece of paper that has to do with either the clinic or the rescue comes across my desk. I send everything to the accountant. I know that your donations barely cover the cost of food and supplies for the rescue. If not for donations from the clinic, and your own pocketbook, the rescue would be in big trouble." She shook her head. "The rescue needs the clinic and they both need this building."

"You're the one who told me I should step up and be a boss, Nolie. Remember that book?"

"I do. And you've done an exemplary job, Doc. The secret is to know that accepting help isn't a sign of weakness. This is a greater cause than your pride."

Everything Nolie said about the rescue was true. They were facts that she'd been well aware of since the day Tucker said he was leaving. Yet, somehow, they'd become muddled in her pursuit to prove she could do the job when he walked out the door.

This had become personal.

Jena plopped down in a chair. "You're right."

"Of course I am. There are very few advantages to being old. Having gone around the block once or twice is one of them."

Silence stretched for several moments. The only sound was the annoying tapping of Nolie's fingernails on the table.

"Mind if I ask you a question, Dr. Harper?"

Jena raised her brows. Why not? Could this day get any worse?

"What about you and Dr. Rainbolt? You two are perfect for each other. How come two very smart people can't figure out what's clear as day to the rest of us?"

"*What? No.* This is Tucker Rainbolt we're talking about. He's like a ten on the scale. I'm maybe a five on a good day." Jena nodded to herself. Enough daydreams about almost-kisses. The facts were the facts. "He's my friend, Nolie, and that's good enough for me."

But was it? Was it really? Being Tucker's BFF wasn't what kept her tossing and turning at night. No, it was the prayer that somehow, he might see how much she cared and feel the same way.

Nolie massaged her forehead. "You're trying my patience, Dr. Harper."

The chimes on the front door sounded, and they both turned their heads. "I better get back to the front desk," Nolie said.

"Wait." Jena placed a hand on the older woman's arm. "Thank you."

"Yes, ma'am." Nolie smiled. "I'll tell you what, maybe we can compromise here. If you'll talk to Dr. Rainbolt, I'll do my best not to eavesdrop again."

Jena rolled her eyes.

"I said I'd try."

A few minutes later, Nolie was knocking on Jena's office door. "Dr. Hardy is here to see you."

Finn Hardy? Just who she didn't need to see. Jena pulled up the appointment calendar on her phone. "Did I miss a scheduled appointment?"

"No, ma'am. He said it won't take but a minute, and I do believe he's gotten cuter since I last saw him."

"Send him in, Nolie, and while you're reforming, could you also *try* not to assess the men who come in and out of the office?"

"Probably not." She strode down the hall, her heels clicking on the linoleum.

"Jena, hi. I'm sorry to interrupt." Finn peeked his head in. There was a smile on his face and the dark eyes sparkled with good humor. Nolie was right again. He was a cute guy. Unfortunately, he was the wrong cute guy.

Still, she couldn't help but smile in return as she stood to greet him. "Hi, there. Come on in. Have a seat."

"I stopped by for two reasons. First, I wanted to thank you for the tickets to Jingle Paws. I had a great time and met some nice people. So much so that I don't want to come to work for you. I'd like to buy the equine practice."

Jena's jaw sagged. "Really? Did you speak to Tucker?"

"I did and put in an offer. He said to talk to you, which is why I'm here." Finn raised his palms. "Are you good with it?"

Things were falling into place, paving the way for Tucker to leave Rebel. She recalled her speech to Finn at the diner. Jena wanted the best for Tucker. That remained the only thing that hadn't changed since he first told her he wanted to move to Texas.

"I'm thrilled," she said. "You're qualified, you're a nice guy and this will be one more thing off my plate."

"Nice guy?" He cringed. "Story of my life."

"That was your takeaway?"

"It did stand out. Especially when I planned to invite you to dinner."

"Oh, Finn, I couldn't. I don't want to give you the wrong idea. You really are a terrific guy and the women in this town will be standing in line to get your attention."

Finn bowed his head, and then slowly lifted his eyes to hers. "Does he know?"

"Know what?" Her heart began to hammer so loudly that she feared Finn could hear.

"That you're in love with him," he murmured.

Jena inhaled sharply and her gaze flew to his. How could he possibly know?

"It's okay, Jena. Your secret is safe with me. Tucker Rainbolt is a mighty blessed man. I hope he figures that out real quick."

She did, too, because as things stood, it looked to her as though she hadn't learned from her mistakes. Once again, she was in love with a man who would walk away without a glance over his shoulder.

"I'm concerned about you, Tuck," Reece said.

"I share his concern," Mitch added. He shoveled a forkful of lemon meringue pie into his mouth and stared at Tucker.

"This is like the Three Stooges in my home," Tucker muttered. He pushed his plate away.

"Are you going to finish that pie?" Reece asked.

Tucker slid the dish across the table to his brother.

"Here I bring my wife's pie to your house, on Sunday no less, and you don't eat it. What's wrong with you, man?" Mitch asked.

"In the tradition of the Rainbolt brothers, Tucker is love struck and in the doghouse at the same time. Well played."

"If it means he's staying in Rebel, I'm good with it," Mitch said. "Besides, I like Jena."

"Yeah, me, too." Reece shook his head. "Can't hardly believe she fell for him, though."

"Do you think she did?" Mitch said.

Tucker's head jerked up at his brother's last words. Did Jena care for him? Maybe not as much as he cared for her. And maybe he was delusional, thinking they had something to build on, when they didn't.

"What are you going to do about your situation?" Mitch asked. He pointed an accusing fork at Tucker. "Go on and apologize and tell her how you feel. It's the only way, and you best get it done soon. Christmas is a week away. The family has plans in the works. You do not want to mess with Daisy and Claire's plan."

"And Kate's coming home," Reece added.

"What does Christmas have to do with anything?" Tucker asked.

"Peace on earth. Goodwill to man," Mitch said. "I would hope that after sitting in the pew every Sunday for most of your life, you might have learned something. Like how to humble yourself and make things right with the woman you love."

"I have no evidence that she has…feelings. I'm functioning on a prayer. A holiday prayer."

"Prayers are good. They're what got me married," Mitch said.

"Speaking of an answer to prayer," Reece said. "I ran into Finn Hardy at church this morning. He told me that he bought the equine clinic. How come you didn't tell me about that?"

"I've had a few other things on my mind."

"Like what?" Reece asked.

"Like interviewing at OSU. Our very own little brother will be part-time faculty at the OSU School of Veterinary Medicine," Mitch said.

"What? How did that happen?" Reece asked. He looked back and forth between his brothers.

Tucker inclined his head toward Mitch.

"Happy to interfere," Mitch said.

Reece slapped a hand on the table. "This is great news."

"Pipe down," Tucker said. "The girls are sleeping."

"I'm grateful you've come to your senses," Reece said softly.

Mitch smiled slow and steady. "This is the best Christmas present the Rainbolts could have. We'll all be together to bring in the New Year. The Lord sure is good."

"Yeah, He is," Reece said.

Tucker nodded. Despite his current situation with Jena, he was grateful, as well. This was where he belonged. It didn't matter that Mitch had interfered by calling the college or that Reece went behind his back and brought in his vet friend. Nope. What mattered is that Tucker didn't want to move to Texas.

He wanted Jena Harper and a life together with his family in Rebel.

Tucker grabbed his coat from the back of the chair and headed for the front door.

"Where are you going?" Mitch asked.

"You can't leave," Reece called after him. "Who's going to watch the girls when they wake up?"

"I guess my big brothers are. I've got groveling to do."

Tucker drove straight to Jena's house and sat in his truck drumming his hands on the steering wheel while working up the courage to get out of the vehicle. The blinking Christmas lights on Jena's house beat out a pattern. He was pretty sure they were mocking him in some secret holiday code.

He sighed.

How difficult could it be? All he had to do was convince Jena that he cared about her. Make her understand that how he felt wasn't about the clinic or the rescue—it was about her.

She was plenty mad about the building. So he'd have to find a way to help her see around that. Buying that building was for their future in Rebel.

Forever.

He liked the sound of that. But would Jena?

Snow had begun to fall on his windows, blocking his view of the house, a sure sign that it was time. He grabbed the gaily wrapped package on the seat next to him and walked up to Jena's door. Before he could ring the bell, the door flew open and Ernie rushed out, tangling her leash around Tucker's legs and knocking him to the ground and the package into the air.

"I've got it," Jena called out. She caught the flying box and turned around. "Tucker!"

In an instant, she was at his side. "Are you all right?"

"Once again, I landed on my hindsight." He sat up. "Jena, listen to me. I need you to know that I bought the building because I want to save the clinic and the rescue. For us." He paused to catch his breath. "We're a team, Jena. A change of plans isn't a failure on your part if we're in this together."

His heart pounded as he waited for her to say something. Anything.

Eyes dark with emotion, Jena frowned. "You're leaving, Tucker."

"No. I'm not."

"What did you say?" Her expression faltered, giving him hope.

"When I went to Texas this time, I turned down the job." He'd thank Reece for that another day.

Ernie looked from Jena to him and licked Tucker's face. "Thanks, girl." He gently rubbed the dog's ears.

"Why did you go then?" Jena asked.

"I wanted to do it proper. Those folks treated me well. I've spent the time since I got back trying to undo all the plans I made to move."

She smiled. It was a smile filled with such joy that he thought…he hoped, that what he saw in her brown eyes meant he had a chance, after all. "You're not leaving?" she repeated.

He shook his head.

"You're staying in Rebel."

"The Lord has given me my heart's desire, right here in Rebel. But I guess I had to figure that out for myself." He heard the ache in his own voice as he spoke. His heart was on the line right now.

"What about Finn Hardy?" Jena asked.

"What about him?" Tucker fairly growled. He was starting to regret bringing the vet to town. Finn Hardy was getting way too much stage time. The guy was supposed to be a walk-on and here he was in the middle of the most important conversation of Tucker's life.

"Tucker, Finn bought the equine clinic," Jena said.

"Yeah, and I'm grateful for that because I've got plans."

"Plans?"

"I'm going to slow down a bit, maybe teach a few classes at the college in Stillwater, enjoy my girls and my new wife."

"Your new wife?" Jena's eyes widened.

"Oh, wait. I forgot to ask you to marry me." He scrambled to his feet and handed her Ernie's leash.

Jena inhaled sharply and her jaw sagged. She glanced at the slightly worse for wear package in her other hand. "What's in the box?"

"It's not a ring, I'm not that organized. It's the director's cut of *It's a Wonderful Life*. I thought we could analyze it together."

"That's so sweet."

Around them, snow fell gently, and the Jingle Paws pup chased the flakes as they danced in the air before finally spiraling to the ground.

"I love you, Jena." He took her mittened hand. "It's as simple as that. You light up a part of me I didn't even know was dark."

"Oh, Tucker. I love you, too."

"You do?" He didn't know what else to say in response.

"Tucker, I've loved you for a long time. I just didn't know it." She sighed. "And then I didn't think I deserved your love."

He chuckled. "For better or for worse. We deserve each other." His heart pounded as he looked into the eyes of the woman he loved so much. "Jena Harper, will you marry me?"

She released a chilly breath that floated into the air. "Yes."

Tucker inclined his head to meet Jena's lips. They were warm and soft, even as the snow continued to fall. Ernie barked, but Tucker was in no hurry. He'd waited a very long time for this kiss.

Epilogue

One Year Later

Jena absently ran her fingers over the beaded bodice of her A-line wedding dress. She willed herself not to panic as she stared at herself in the full-length mirror.

"I don't even look like me. This is some sort of holiday hallucination."

"I thought you loved that dress," Dee said from behind her.

"I do, but is it me? Is this Jena Harper?"

"It's so you." Dee smiled.

"Why did I think I could pull off a Christmas wedding?"

"Jena, you did pull it off. The chapel is decorated like a Christmas tree. Red velvet bows are tied to the pews, along with strands of white pearls wrapped around fresh fir garlands." Dee smiled. "The reception hall is stunning, as well.

Tucker put the tree up and it's lit with tiny white lights. Everything is perfect."

"What if no one comes?" Jena asked. Panic rising, she lifted the chiffon skirt and headed to the door of the bridal room.

"Where are you going?" Dee's voice held a trace of panic as she picked up the tulle of her forest green maid of honor dress and followed.

"I just want to peek into the chapel."

"That is not a good idea, Dr. Harper," Nolie called out.

"I want to go with Aunty Jena," Hazel said. The five-year-old adjusted her red flower girl dress and started across the room.

"Me, too! Me, too!" Ginger scrambled to find her other white patent-leather Mary Jane.

"She'll be right back," Nolie said. She held Claire's four-month-old baby girl to her shoulder as she guarded the door. "Won't you, Dr. Harper?"

"Yes, absolutely my sweet girls," Jena called as she started down the hall.

Jena's bridesmaids, Kate, Daisy and Claire, rushed after the bride in their holiday-themed bridesmaid dresses. Red tulle skirts swished as all three headed down the hall, as well.

"The dog! Don't let Ernie out!" Nolie cried as she reached for her beribboned collar with a free hand.

Jena carefully opened the side door of the chapel and peeked inside. Heart thudding, she released a small gasp. Every seat in the small Rebel Ranch chapel was filled. Pastor Tuttle stood at the altar, ready to perform the ceremony. He looked up and smiled at Jena. She offered a weak smile in return and closed the door.

"Is the entire town of Rebel, Oklahoma, out there?" Jena asked.

"Probably," Daisy said.

"Along with Rainbolt friends from Tulsa and Pawhuska," Claire added.

"My father is here," Dee said. "It was so nice of you to send him an invitation."

"Well, he's family, too." Jena turned and smiled tenderly at her daughter, whose hair was a deep chocolate brown, like her mother's, and pulled into an elegant chignon for the wedding.

The Rainbolt family was growing. With Dee and the new baby, that made close to twenty.

Twenty Rainbolts and a full chapel.

Jena quickly walked back to the bridal room. She stood at the window, staring out at the snow-covered pastures of Rebel Ranch, collecting her thoughts. But instead of the white pastoral landscape, she kept seeing the chapel filled with people, as the hum of their excited voices echoed in her head.

"I don't know if I can do this," she whispered. "There are so many people."

"Yes, there are a lot of people," Dee said. "They all love you and Tucker, Jena."

Daisy whispered to Claire, *"Go get Tucker. Hurry."*

It was only minutes before she felt Tucker's breath warming her neck and heard him whisper her name near her ear.

"Jena?"

The tension she'd been wearing like a cloak fell away at his words.

She whirled around and caught her breath at the sight of him. "Tucker. You look so handsome." Jena ran a hand over the fabric of his lapel, stopping to admire his boutonniere, a white rosebud with a sprig of fresh pine. Her gaze moved to the strong jawline and the steady blue eyes that never wavered.

Tucker kissed her forehead while Nolie quickly ushered everyone out of the room, even Ernie.

"And you..." His gaze caressed her face. "Wow, I've never seen anything prettier than you at this moment."

Jena's face warmed. "You aren't supposed to see the bride before the wedding."

"We don't believe that stuff, do we? You and I have so much more than silly superstitions."

Jena nodded, her heart overflowing with emotion. They did. So much more.

"Tell me what's going on," he urged. "You don't want to get married?"

She looked into his eyes and saw nothing but love. "I want to get married."

"Then?"

"All those people, Tucker."

"All those people who love us, Jena. We can't deny them an opportunity to be blessed by what the good Lord has done for us."

Jena blinked as she processed his words. "I never thought of it that way."

"The animals of Rebel have brought us an extended family. That family wants to see our happily-ever-after. Besides, the ceremony only takes a little time, and then we have that amazing Luna Diaz meal waiting at the reception hall." Tucker winked.

"She's making those little dim sums for us."

"So let's give the Lord thanks in His house and then we can eat."

"Okay. Yes, you're right."

"He'll never leave you, Jena. And neither will I. I'm here forever." He looked at her and frowned. "Are you wearing heels?"

She nodded. "Three inches. I want to make it easier to kiss you. But I brought my high-tops for the reception."

Tucker dipped his head. When his mouth touched hers, she was lost. "My beloved is mine and I am his." She whispered the words of Solomon against his lips.

With a knock on the door, Nolie peeked her head in. "Doctors, it's time."

Tucker kissed her forehead. "I'm going to get going. I'll see you in a few minutes. I'll be the tall guy with the big grin, because he's been blessed to find love a second time."

Jena smiled and put her hand to her heart as she willed herself not to cry and ruin her makeup.

"Ready?" Dee asked.

"I am."

The processional began with the bridesmaids: Daisy, followed by Claire and then Kate.

Her maid of honor and daughter, Dee, was next.

"It's your turn, girls," Nolie prompted from the side.

Jena's new daughters, Hazel and Ginger, smiled at each other as they walked onto the carpeted chapel aisle, each holding red and green satin ribbons tied to Ernie's collar.

"Here you go," Nolie said. She handed Jena the bridal bouquet of fresh Christmas greenery and white roses.

"Thank you, Magnolia," Jena whispered.

Nolie nodded and wiped away a tear.

The chiffon dress billowed as Jena stepped forward to take Mitch Rainbolt's arm.

"Ready, Jena?" Mitch whispered.

"Yes," she breathed. They moved slowly toward the altar, past a blur of people.

Today she was marrying her best friend.

Thank You, Lord, for Tucker and the Rainbolt family, and for the people of Rebel. Amen.

Head raised, she kept her eyes on Tucker. Oh, how much she loved this precious man who gave her so much and loved her unconditionally.

When Tucker smiled back at her, it occurred to Jena that she had been absolutely correct. Happily ever after was the new Rainbolt family motto.

* * * * *

*If you enjoyed this story,
don't miss Tina Radcliffe's next
sweet romance,
available next year from Love Inspired!*

*Find more great reads at
www.LoveInspired.com*

Dear Reader,

I can't believe we're already releasing the third book of the Hearts of Oklahoma series. I absolutely love all of the Rainbolts, but this book is very special. Digging deep to portray the authentic and complex emotions of the characters in this story was admittedly hard work, though well worth it. I really came to love Tucker and Jena. As a side note, Nolie Parker was a character who surprised me at every turn with her sassiness.

It was only fitting that animals like Ernie and Chester played a primary role in this story, as animals provide their humans unconditional love. And how fitting to set a story about second chances and unconditional love during the holiday season.

Merry Christmas, dear reader. Thank you for sharing this journey to Rebel, Oklahoma, with me. As usual, you can find many of the tasty holiday recipes from this book on my website at www.tinaradcliffe.com

I look forward to hearing from you.

Sincerely,
Tina Radcliffe

Get 4 FREE REWARDS!

We'll send you 2 FREE Books plus <u>2 FREE Mystery Gifts.</u>

Harlequin Heartwarming Larger-Print books will connect you to uplifting stories where the bonds of friendship, family and community unite.

FREE
Value Over
$20